Rebecca's Flame

Lynne Kositsky

Cover by Carol Biberstein

The Canada Council | Le Conseil des Arts
for the Arts | du Canada
since 1957 | depuis 1957

We acknowledge the support of the Canada
Council for the Arts for our publishing program.

We acknowledge the financial support of the Government
of Canada through the Book Publishing Industry
Development Program for publishing activities.

All rights reserved.

No part of this publication may be reproduced or stored in a retrieval system, or
transmitted in any form or by any means, electronic, mechanical, photocopying,
recording, or otherwise, without prior written permission of the publisher. For
information: Roussan Publishers Inc.,
2110 Decarie Blvd., Suite 100, Montreal QC H4A 3J3 Canada or
P.O. Box 156, Schuyler Falls NY 12985 USA

http://www.roussan.com

Copyright ©1998 by Lynne Kositsky

National Library of Canada
Bibliothèque nationale du Québec

Canadian Cataloguing in Publication Data
Kositsky, Lynne, 1947-
Rebecca's flame
(On time's wing)
ISBN 1-896184-56-1

I. Famines-Ireland-History-19th century-Juvenile fiction. 2. Quebec (Province)-
Emigration and immigration-Juvenile fiction. I. Title. II. Series.

PS8571.O85R42 1999   jC813'.54   C99-900920-6
PZ7.K689Re 1999

Interior design by Jean Shepherd
Cover by Carol Biberstein
Cover design by Dan Clark

Published simultaneously in Canada and the United States of America
Printed in Canada

Typeface Minion

1 2 3 4 5 6 7 8 9 Gagné 8 7 6 5 4 3 2 1 0 9

For Michael

Acknowledgements: Thanks to Cathy Stein and Menachem Goldstein for advice on Jewish customs; Patrick O. Young for advice on Irish Gaelic; the guides and interpreters of Grosse Isle for taking me around the island in the pouring rain; Dan Griffin and Eddie Conway of Shannon for their historical insights; Karen and Jean-Marie Allard, Joy Daniels and Marlene Matthews for their help and support; Jane Frydenlund for being such a fabulous editor; and my family and friends for putting up with me.

Author's note: Rebecca lives in an imaginary city which somewhat resembles Dublin, but I have taken the liberty of borrowing geographical and historical detail from the west coast of Ireland, where the famine hit hardest. The first two years of the famine, 1845 and 1846, are spliced together for dramatic effect.

1

To begin at the beginning, which was the start of the end for some—a famine came upon the land. Not the hot desert starvation known to the pharaohs, but a wet disaster more akin to Noah's flood. The catastrophe arrived slowly, so slowly at first that it was hardly noticeable. A warm spring and a hot summer, the promise of plentiful harvest, gave way little by little to sparse drizzle, then rain and gloom, and afterwards such a relentless downpour that what was left of the crop sickened and lay like blackened scum on the earth.

But I go beyond what I had meant to say for, truly, we in the towns did not understand the enormity of the problem at first, although there was flooding enough to sink the ark. How could we know that such a small thing as a month or two of rain would be the beginning of a tragedy that would alter our lives forever? Our existence may have been changing on a level almost invisible to us, but meanwhile time went on very much in its usual pattern, though we were dreadfully inconvenienced by the wet.

I could not go to the shops without my shawl and skirt getting soaked, without wearing clogs over my shoes in the muddy laneways. Nor could I wander the hills and meadows outside the town when my chores were finished and my older sister Sarah was quiet. In vain did I regret the days when Ireland was washed only by spring sunshine, and the emerald grass flourished between the ancient grey walls and stony outcroppings that divided the fields. Green and grey, that is how I thought of my new country. But now only grey, as the dirty rain fell and fell from the drowned heavens onto the drowned earth, and our house was as damp as a *mikvah*, a ritual bath.

It took me a full hour in the morning to get the fire under the stove to draw. All the while, I would watch to ensure Sarah did not burn herself on one of the spills I was using to bring the flame from the fireplace, or find some other mischief to drag me from my task. That meant breakfast was late, so my father was rough tempered as a sailor who had drunk the night away down at the docks, though he never touched a drop except a cup of wine well prayed on during the Sabbath.

"Rebecca," he would roar, his grey grizzled beard trembling with rage and his skullcap almost toppling from his head, "food, now! How can I perform morning prayers on an empty stomach? And take your sister upstairs and dress her. I will not have her running around in a shift." I would screech the metal pot across the stove and slide oatmeal into bowls on the big polished table, before dragging my sister up to corset and petticoat her. I could not fault her for trying to evade her stays. The whalebone was as taut and painful against our flesh as a horse whip, and I would have avoided it also had I dared.

I tried to pull Sarah into her drawers and dress as she laughed and sang, falling forward, swinging her arms out in front of her like a Dutch windmill. Not that she was always like that. No, sometimes she would be serious enough to read or sit at needlework, and occasionally she would lie in her bed and refuse to get up. God forgive me, but I prayed for the days she lay under the bedclothes, sobbing quietly to herself. At least, then, she was little trouble. How I wished that my mother still lived, or at least that we were back in Poland, despite all its dangers, with the company of others of our own kind, and a girl who came in to help with the cooking and other tasks. Now I had to do all the chores except the washing, watch my sister constantly, and even fasten my own corsets, which was an almost impossible task since I faced the other way. Once and once only had I asked Sarah to help, and she laced me to the bed post, escaping quickly down the back stairs and out into the town, laughing through her long fair hair as she went.

Father did his best to ignore Sarah's situation, remarking every so often, frustrated in his praying or accounting, that she was a lunatic and leaving it at that. I knew there was something terribly wrong with her, but winced at Father's term. Whenever he said it my mind went to restraints and straitjackets at the Bethlem Hospital in England, and I would resolve to look after her better. I could not bear to think of her chained in some dirty cell somewhere, not my sister, my closest kin, force-fed strange potions to vomit up the evil spirits that held her spellbound. When I was small and she was still well, she had looked after me, wiping my face and dressing me, taking the part of our mother. Now we had switched roles. At fifteen I was my eighteen-year-old sister's caretaker. I hoped fervently that in the end the evil spirits would leave her, and she would settle down and come right. I prayed nightly that it might be so.

The New Year, *Rosh Hashanah*, came and went, as did the Day of Atonement. In many ways everything took its normal and familiar course. I had managed to obtain a fat chicken for the New Year's holiday from a man who was giving up his farm, and its succulent smell reminded me of times past, in Poland. On *Yom Kippur* we fasted, and it made our meal taste all the better afterwards. But I was beginning to have a problem obtaining foodstuffs, particularly fresh vegetables, from the shopkeepers. And Heaven help me if there were no potatoes on the table at dinnertime, though they were selling for seven pence or more a pound.

The rain stopped after the High Holidays, and we pushed our wares to the market the next Saturday, my clogs and Sarah's clacking over slippery cobbled streets still slick from the flooding. Father and I laid our ribbons, cheap bracelets, and other trinkets on a long cloth-covered barrow, where whatever watery rays there were would find them. The more expensive jewellery we left at the shop, for we could not risk it among the poor and quick-fingered market folk. I eyed our merchandise with disgust, having argued over and over with Father about trading on the Sabbath, when the Lord said we should rest. But he replied only, "God will forgive us. We have to make a living."

My father's brand of religion confused me. How was it that I had to keep our food kosher, separate the milk and meat plates, and fast on Yom Kippur but could sell on the Sabbath without blinking so much as an eyelash? It appeared we could be good Jews as long as our observances didn't lessen our earnings. However, if my duty to Father was different from my duty to God, I knew to obey the former first, blasphemous though that might sound. I understood Father's punishment to be harsher and swifter, although later, as our immediate world sank into want and chaos, I would wonder if I had been right. As the months passed, my father's trade would disappear like seeds on the wind, and his face would grow gaunt, more from anger and disappointment than from hunger. But what did we know of that then?

I tied Sarah's wrist to mine with a string when we left the house, but she soon bit through it and disappeared. Father vanished, too, apparently to search for her, more likely to converse with Mr. Cohen, the only other Jew who plied his wares in the market. I was left to my own devices and stood expecting the usual rush of customers. They would turn our wares over and over in their grubby hands, fingering everything, buying a piece of flash here, a bit of glitter there.

Still, there was something different about this place today, something that made me hug my shawl around me tighter and sink into myself: fewer stalls and customers, a rotten foreboding of disease, and an almost acrid stench around the pitifully small mounds of vegetables, mostly withered cabbages and turnips from the previous winter. Hardly a potato to be seen, and what there was lay blackened and soft as the rubbish on a midden. How would people get through the year if there was so little left to eat at harvest time? There were still fish to be sure, laid out in their silver and rainbow hues on the stalls, but their price was too dear for most.

It wasn't so bad for us. Father had money put away against disaster, and there was always food to be had if one possessed the wherewithal. But even our family would not eat as well as usual and, if that were so, what would happen to the poor? They barely managed to survive during good years. I had already seen plenty of thin, ragged women and children around the market begging, particularly in the hungry summer months when the potatoes were all eaten. Often I tried to slip them a coin or two when Father was busy elsewhere. What would happen to them if times grew even worse? The truth of it was, I had never seen such poverty before—not in Poland, not in London where we had lived for some years before coming to Ireland. I understood only too well there was nothing extra for these people to live off in mean seasons. As if to underscore my dread, two men walked past me, talking in low voices.

"My potatoes still sit in the fields. A blight came upon them before I could dig them out of the ground," whispered the first, as if hatching a plot. "And so beautiful the plants looked in June, you'd have reckoned there to be a fine crop."

"I heard say that you can bury the good ones and dig them up later. Or, if you grate the blighted potatoes into water, you can separate the starch and eat it in puddings," replied the second, scratching his scabby neck and squinting around as though he guarded a great secret. I lowered my eyes.

"Wouldn't want to touch anything that came from those potatoes. No, mark my words, man, we're all for the poorhouse by winter. It's the landlords to blame."

The men moved out of earshot. How could the landlords be condemned for rain and blight? Surely it was God's will to bring plague and pestilence upon us? But now a dirty youth with spider-leg fingers was standing at my barrow, running his hands over the goods and grinning to himself. I had seen him before, and often when he left I could swear that an item of merchandise disappeared with him.

"Away with you," I told him. "I have no time for you today. I wish only for paying customers."

"Then you won't be wanting to know that your sister upset the baker's cart and has run away with one of his best pork pies. The baker's raced after her with a big stick, and she stands in the square gibing at him and stuffing pig down her gullet."

Without thought of the consequences I was away, running across the market. What was worse? That Sarah had stolen or that she had eaten pig, *tref*? Or that the baker was after her and would probably make mincemeat of her for his Christmas tarts? I looked everywhere, darting hither and thither across the square. My sister was nowhere to be found, although I did eventually come across the baker, calmly hawking his breads and pies. Knowing immediately I'd been had by Spider Fingers, I rushed back to my barrow, but it was too late. He was gone, and a goodly number of my cheap jewels were gone also.

All traces of the sun had suddenly disappeared, and tongues of mist licked at the corners of the market, blurring the images of stalls and people. The small, sharp splashes of colour on a gown or hatband were rapidly dissolving into the fog, and sound wrapped itself into a soft spiral, falling away in the enveloping greyness. I felt completely alone, as if the day and the market had disappeared into a halo of low cloud.

"God in Heaven, how could I be so stupid?" I moaned into the fog, twisting my narrow gold ring around my finger, as I always did when upset. I would never find the boy now. He had vanished into the haze, and even if I did manage to corner him, how could I pry our jewellery from him? The loss was not great in monetary terms, but Father would almost certainly say it was a telling example of my carelessness, and I would be punished in some pathetic, humiliating fashion, made to wash the household linens myself or scrub the floors twice over.

"Yours, I believe." A soft voice penetrated the mist, and I turned quickly. Standing before me was a youth of about my own age, or perhaps a year older. He was what the people thereabouts called black Irish: hair of jet with a bluish tinge to it and eyes of the darkest grey, tiny lines radiating from them like sunbeams. His skin, though, was milk white, far fairer than mine and finer, too. He was also a Gentile, most likely a Catholic, a poor Catholic judging by his threadbare clothing. I stepped back abruptly, almost tripping over the barrow as he held out a handful of bracelets.

"Come, you may take them," he said gently. "Didn't I rescue

them for you from that dreadful boy who hangs around the stalls and steals whatever he can lay his long skinny fingers on? But for sure I disappointed him this time."

"Thank you. You have no idea the favour you've done me." I could barely look at him as I took the proffered jewellery and put it back in its place.

"'Twas nothing." His smile cut like sunshine through the gloom. I put my hand out to the handle of the barrow to steady myself and took a deep breath. I was meaning to reply, but couldn't speak as I gazed into the dark eyes that reflected my own.

"Those ribbons are pretty as the day," he went on, glancing down at my wares and changing the subject as if tacking a ship. "I'm wishing I could afford them for my sisters."

"Please, take them as a just reward," I replied, relieved I had found my voice at last. "It would be a little enough gift for the trouble you have put yourself to."

"No, never would I do that, but I could barter for them if you have a mind."

"In exchange for what?" This was a mistake. I knew it as soon as the words flew from my mouth.

"For your gracious favour...and a few hens' eggs brought to your house fresh on the morning they're laid."

The latter was an offer too good to pass up. Although I was covered with confusion by what he had just said, I minded well that an egg was far more useful currency than a whole wagon of flattery. I glanced up at him shyly and smiled. "That would indeed be a fair exchange."

"Let me know where you live then, young Miss, and they'll be at your door before you've polished the front step."

What was more dangerous? I wondered in bed that night. That I had accepted the compliments of a Gentile, or that I had given out our street and house name? Perhaps this last was even worse than the possibility of Sarah eating pig. In any case, I had told him our address loudly and clearly, barking it out as bold as any fishwife in the stalls, and he had vanished like a wraith into the fog just as Father returned. I found Sarah sitting at the well with her skirts drawn up to her thighs and her feet dangling down towards the water. Tethering her to me once again, I pushed the barrow up the street past the castle to home.

2

We had sold nothing that day, and Father was in a foul temper the next morning, banging his fist upon the table and upsetting his oatmeal. My own mood was not much better. I had dreamed all night of armies of poor skinny wretches standing in the flooded furrows next to the potato ridges, spading the sopping earth back over the new-grown seedlings. These creatures then waited, patient yet forlorn, until their flesh fell away from their bones and they crumbled into a heavy black fog which hung over the fields. Waking at midnight with my heart near bursting in my breast, I had hastened down to the scullery to fetch a cup of water from the pail. But when I returned to sleep, the tragic armies pursued me. They scrambled over one another in the rain, their faces featureless, their long hook-nailed fingers thrust forward like bayonets. With a terrible conviction, I knew I had seen the future.

The youth did not come. I had prayed that he would not appear until Father departed for the shop, forgetting it was Sunday and Father was home all day, but he did not materialize at all. Perhaps it was a blessing. Yet all the same, I felt cheated and lonely as I scrubbed and polished the house, prepared the evening meal.

"I have no friends here, Father," I remarked at supper, as I served up the soup.

"Nonsense. You have Shmuel Cohen from the market, and your sister."

"Mr. Cohen is three times my age, if not four. He is your friend perhaps, but not mine. And my sister at the moment is not fit to be anybody's friend, even her own." I glanced at Sarah. She had calmed down in no little measure, but was now rocking backwards and forwards on her chair as though praying, and sighing as though she had witnessed the end of the world.

Father was not willing to relent. "Still, there are the Benaris," he said, wagging his finger at me. "Remember the Benaris? They have a daughter close to you in years."

"Judita is nine, Father, barely nine years old. And the Benaris speak no Yiddish and barely any English at all. They rattle on in some foreign tongue thirteen to the dozen, and I can scarcely squeeze a word through the cracks in their chatter. They give me a headache."

"They are Sephardic, Rebecca, Marranos, and all of their kind have endured terrible trials. Converted to Christianity on pain of death or thrust out of Spain, wandering from place to place through the centuries. And despite all, they lit the Sabbath candles secretly, their true religion a flame which burnt hot and true in their hearts."

This was a story I'd heard many times before. "I know Father, and I have great respect for them. They're just not friends, not close friends, that is."

"Will I ever be done with whining women?" replied my father

irritably, getting up and going to sit by the fire. "I'll take the rest of my meal here, Rebecca. And don't stint with the meat, if you please."

"And I cannot imagine forsaking Judaism for any reason," I muttered, too low for him to hear. As I dished meat and vegetables onto Father's plate, giving him his own and some of the meat I had reserved for my portion, the knock I had been awaiting all day echoed through the house.

"Now, who could this be so late on a Sunday evening?" asked my father angrily. He hated anything that disrupted routine.

"I'll get it, Father," I replied breathlessly, thrusting his meal at him. "You're settled so comfortably there." Without waiting for his answer, I ran through the front hall to the door, unbolting and opening it in a single movement. The night air, clear and cold, rushed into the house, and I gathered my shawl tighter around me.

"Well there you are, Rebecca, at last, and me half frozen to death on your front step." It was, as I had surmised, the black-haired boy, as large as life and twice as miraculous. Three fat eggs were clutched in one hand as though nested there. His cap sat in the other.

"Put your cap back on then. And how in Heaven do you know my name?"

"Didn't I hear your father call you by it just yesterday at the market, and that's the truth of it. Here are your eggs. A brown, a speckled, and a white, just like the Holy Trinity."

I took them from his hand, trying to ignore the pointed reference to Christianity. His fingers, cold as icicles, touched mine and made me jump. Moonlight glimmered in his hair.

"There, I'm not that frightening, am I?" he smiled. "I promise not to hurt you. And now for your part of the bargain."

I put the eggs down carefully on the small table in the hall, pulling several ribbons from my pocket where I'd been keeping them all day in anticipation of such a meeting. As I thrust them at him nervously, a pale pink one snaked through my hand onto the floor.

"Sure, and I was hoping for the other portion of your payment," he said as he bent to retrieve it. I had not noticed till then how shockingly thin he was, and I was brought to mind of my dream of the night before. Could he be one of the poverty-stricken who would pursue the fortunate, die of starvation in the fields? Now there was something, an emotion both complicated and dangerous, that stood between us and sucked the breath from me.

"And what was that?" I whispered, remembering myself, my lips dry as kindling and barely capable of forming words.

"Your gracious favour, Becca." He rose again and looked straight into my eyes, his lilting brogue disarming my powerful fancy. No one had ever asked for my favour before, and certainly no one had called me Becca, a name that tripped light and silken off the boy's tongue. Sarah called me Becky, a nickname I hated, if she was well enough to notice me at all. Father used my full formal name, which, by his tone, always sounded as though he were annoyed with me.

As if to accentuate the point, my father's voice boomed from the back room, "Come along in, Rebecca, and shut the front door. You're heating the whole outside, and God knows fuel is expensive."

"I have to go," I whispered in a panic to the boy.

"Won't you first let me make my excuses for the late call? The truth is my sister Bridget was ill, I had to go to church, our last remaining hen wouldn't lay, and..."

But I never heard the end of his apology. My father was suddenly in the hall and standing between us. "What's this? What's this?" he bellowed, almost apoplectic at seeing his daughter talking to a strange Gentile on the doorstep.

I hardly knew how to address the problem. "Father," I stuttered, twisting my ring, "This is...this is..." and I stopped in confusion. I didn't even know the boy's name.

"Sean, Sir, Sean Woodlock."

"Hmph," replied Father, straightening his skullcap.

"And here I am late on a Sunday night, bringing your daughter the eggs she ordered at the market. I was clean out of them, wouldn't you know it, yesterday."

"She's paid you, has she?"

"Oh yes, sir." The youth smiled.

"Then your business is concluded, I believe," said Father in his very clipped, correct English. He shut the door and bolted it. I was inside, the boy Sean was out, and perhaps I would never see him again.

3

In this new country, I had three possessions that mattered more to me than anything else: an old peg doll which slept on my coverlet; a miniature of my mother which reposed in my bodice close to my heart; and a violin which lay always inside the downstairs breakfront, in sad want of playing. I was thinking of the last with regret, one day in early October. I had been so taken up with chores of late that I had been unable to practice. But today I was determined to quit the house and carry the instrument to my secret place in the hills. Father, though, clearly had other projects to occupy the precious moments I had allotted to my own activities.

"Dress your sister today. We have company for dinner." I guessed by company he meant Mr. Cohen, who had been spending an excessive amount of time with us lately. A kind old man, though not overly intelligent, his presence would require my cooking all day. In addition, making Sarah decent would involve a desperate struggle. She had lain in bed for weeks and would hardly rouse herself even to use the chamber pot.

"Couldn't you have chosen another day, Father? The stove will be taken up with Mrs. O'Brien's washing all morning."

"Cook in the afternoon then, or over the fire if you have a mind to. It is impossible to change things now." He threw a handful of coins upon the table, put on his great coat, and prepared to leave.

"That's not enough money, Father, if you want a decent meal. Prices have risen enormously these last few weeks."

Throwing another sixpence down, Father left the house, holding the door open at the last moment for Mrs. O'Brien, our washerwoman, to enter. A big, red-faced woman, Mrs. O'Brien cleaned our linens every Monday for a few coppers. To my mind, she was worth her weight in silver bullion.

"Your petticoats are filthy, Miss," she admonished as she scrubbed the first load and put it on to boil in a big cauldron.

"That's because the streets were like quagmires till last week, Mrs. O'Brien. But magical laundress that you are, I'm sure you'll bewitch them clean."

"I'll hang them outside for the sun to bleach. There's a bit of a wind today, m'dear."

I hesitated for a moment as she sorted the sheets and attacked them with kosher soap and a vengeance. Then I drew courage and enquired whether she could keep an eye on Sarah while I went out. "She won't need much looking after, Mrs. O. She barely stirs."

"Don't worry yourself, girl, on that account. I'll care for her like she was me own. But watch yourself on the roads today. There's many a one that shouldn't be around, though I say so m'self. The hunger has brought them in from the country like mice to the cheese, though as to what we shall do with them I have no notion."

She was right. All too frequently the roads were choked with those thrown off their land and starving. They had nowhere to go but the poorhouse, where they would be shamed and separated. Oftentimes, they preferred to die as a family rather than enter its gates. I was angry and frustrated but powerless to help save in small miserable ways that were all but meaningless: a coin here, a scrap of food there. Every time I went out to buy dinner, every time I put the poker to the fire to hasten its flame, a tremendous guilt engulfed me. But then I would forget because of my troublesome workload, and life would go on in its difficult yet familiar ways.

Today I tried not to think of those poor unfortunates, but of the two or three hours liberty Mrs. O'Brien's presence had accorded me. Hastily, I donned my bonnet and cape. Slipping Father's coins and the violin beneath my outer clothing, I let myself out of the back door. My heart ached for the freedom of the hills. From my secret and lofty perch I would gaze down upon the heavy flood-swollen river, the two great cathedrals and castle which dominated the horizon, and feel separate, for a few precious moments, from the city's poverty and grief.

It was surprisingly warm for the time of year, and I soon loosened my bonnet ribbons. How odd that we should have such heat now, when in summer we had experienced nothing except cold weather and flood. God's hand was strong in this reversal of the normal order, I concluded. But why? What had these people done that could possibly be bad enough to deserve the dreadful fate they were facing? And what had I done to escape it? Why were they suffering with such enormity, whilst some of us seemed almost immune to the tragedy? Were we not like the Israelites, whose homes the angel had passed over on his way to kill the Egyptian firstborn?

The smell of the breweries, rotten and over-sweet, hung over the houses, making it difficult to breathe. As long as I lived here, as long as the men needed their beer, I would never grow accustomed to the stench. I continued my walk to the outskirts of the town, where a pitiful family attracted my attention. A mother, father, and four or five dirty children had thrown up a mean shelter on the street. Two heavy-set constables were obliging them, with truncheons and little gentleness, to move on.

"Can they not stay?" I asked one of the men. The mother's face, thin and defeated, haunted me, and I almost wept to see a skeletal baby trying to draw milk from her empty breast.

"No, Miss. Landlord hereabouts says they must move on. You don't need to be troubling yourself with ones such as these, anyway. They're like rats—they'll survive anywhere."

I did not dare argue with the man but doubted heartily that this was so. Drawing my purse from under my cloak and opening the strings carefully, I withdrew more than half the money Father had given me to buy our evening meal. I pressed it on the woman as delicately as I could.

"Thank you, Miss. Good fortune to you," she sighed, her eyes still dull at the sight of the coins. Poor woman, she had endured too much. Or she simply knew, as I did, that these few meagre coppers would stave off want for half a day at most. But it appeared that in trying to help I had made the most dreadful mistake. Within a few seconds there were at least a dozen ragged beggars around me, jostling and crying, thrusting their fingers out to me in a desperate effort to acquire something for themselves.

I was almost thrown to the ground in the confusion. "Please, please, please, I have no more to give," I called to them, much frightened.

One of the constables came to my rescue, pushing the hands away like dry twigs. "See what I mean, Miss? You can't be too careful. Leave this young lady alone now," he went on to the gathering crowd. "Or I'll take care of you m'self." Gradually the people vanished, although one or two of the bolder remained until the man growled nastily and shook his stick at them. They were gone to ground then like hunted animals, and the street was calm once more.

I thanked him and resumed my walk, realizing for the first time how unsafe I was on the streets. The day was excessively hot now, and I would have been glad to shed my cloak. I took the path that led up to the hills, but almost immediately heard footfalls behind me. Worried that the rabble was returning, I quickened my pace. Before I could feel the full fear of my situation, however, someone fell into step beside me, his voice murmuring in my ear, "Becca, my daddy's gone to England to find work, my mam works for the middleman, and I take care of my three young sisters. She's a wonder is Mam—works like a Trojan to put a morsel of food on the table."

"Mr. Woodlock. Sean," I cried out, stopping dead in my tracks with delight.

"The girls are Mary, Peggy and Bridget—she's the baby—and Mary's doing a good job of helping now, as she's gone twelve. My grandparents are long dead," he finished as an afterthought, before gazing at me seriously.

"Why are you telling me this?"

"Because I want you to know everything about me, Becca, every blessed thing. I was about to say that we just killed and ate our last chicken and we're down to a trickle of oatmeal, but I didn't want to sound unduly tragic at first."

I looked at him perplexedly, overwhelmed by his litany of poverty and unsure how to respond. There was the emptiness of silence between us for a moment, and then I pulled out the last coins from my purse, anxious to help.

"I will not take money from you, Becca, not as long as I draw breath." Sean pushed my hand away angrily, his bearing haughty and proud as a lord's. Embarrassed, I turned away and began climbing the hill again.

He soon caught up to me. "But you don't have to worry about us, for the middleman will see there's something in our mouths for as long as Mam's his housekeeper. Sure, it's a hot day and no mistake, and what do you carry with such care under your cloak?"

"How did you come upon me?" I asked, curious, ignoring his question for the moment.

"I did not 'come upon you', as you say, but have followed you all the way up from your house. Wouldn't I have rescued you from the crowd if that crow-garbed constable," and here he spat copiously to the side, "hadn't managed it for me? It's unsafe for you to be abroad, Becca, so I've been keeping my eye on you."

We had reached the summit at last. Sean sat down on the dry spiky grass and, after a moment's hesitation, I took my place beside him, dropping my cloak.

"'Tis a fiddle after all, and me thinking by the way you held it 'twas a baby at the very least. Becca, will you do me one favour, one favour in this world?" He did not wait for a reply but went on: "Take off your bonnet so I can see the full glory of your hair."

My hair, glorious? That great thick swathe that looked like earthy carrots just dug out of the ground? That hung like a bed curtain down my back, refusing to be tamed or fashioned? Sarah's hair was lovely, mine an ugly nuisance. As usual, though, Sean's remark confused me terribly, and I felt a deep blush stain my face.

"It is not proper for you to speak to me that way," I said, jumping up and turning to hide my flushed cheeks.

"Nor is it. But your hair *is* lovely. Like cloth of gold, or a weeping willow bough, downbending into the lake come autumn." He was smiling. I did not, could not understand how to deal with his teasing.

"I must go," I muttered, hurriedly picking up my cloak and violin, and preparing to run down the hill.

"Becca, Becca, I'm not asking you to wed me, merely to show me your long lovely hair. But if 'tis disagreeable to you, forget the words were spoken." Sean stood up and took my arm, steering me to a vantage-point from whence we could gaze on the town. "Look down there. See how the mighty river has fallen now, a spectre of its former self. The flood is all vanished, where it meets the Irish Sea. See along there—no there, my dear, you look in the wrong direction—the majestic Parliament House, and there where Handel first played "Messiah" to the gasping crowds. Is it not the most beautiful, the most important city in the world?"

He stood so close to me that I could feel his quick breath, could see through the holes in his shirt the lean flesh with the shadowy arc of bone beneath. How could I think of the wonders of the town when its people were declining into starvation and death? I told Sean as much, angrily, but he merely replied, "Ireland will outlive its misery, Becca, and rise again, a dignified and powerful land. Did we not rebel against the Vikings, in their time, and the English, too? Now we shall rise against the landlords, perhaps with more success, and take the country for our own once more." He spoke quietly, but with such strength and conviction that I realized I had understood him little until this moment.

"Please, Sean," I begged. "Do not endanger your life."

"I will not, Becca. I have my family to look out for, though I thank you for your concern. But mark me, there are savage times ahead." He stood tall and unbending, gazing out into the distance at the small square fields still spread like black handkerchiefs in mourning over the landscape, the trees sticking up like gibbets. I knew it was useless to address him further on the matter.

The sun shone high in the sky. It was midday, arrived far too quickly. Captivated though I was by Sean's presence, I remembered I had my chores to look to, as well as my sister to take care of. I endeavoured to beg my leave of him. However, he insisted on walking me home, carrying my violin and conversing all the way, even pointing out, before we reached the town, that his house was over yonder. He left me at my door, but once in I realized I had forgotten the shopping. Leaving for it at once, I thought I saw Spider Fingers skulking behind a post. And he was grinning.

4

There were four of us to dinner that night: Father, Mr. Cohen, Sarah, and myself. Mrs. O'Brien had not merely looked after Sarah that morning, she had washed and dressed her. My sister sat at the table now, clean faced and expectant at the thought of food. She looked unexceptional and was perhaps coming into one of those rare periods when she would imitate her former self. Whenever it happened my mind tricked me sadly, for I would believe she was returning to her old naturalness, and we would none of us be burdened with her strange moods and fancies again. But each time I was mistaken. If it happens now, I thought, I will enjoy it for what it is, without thinking she is cured, or that the evil spirits have left her.

As I bustled about the stove after Father had intoned the *Kiddush*, eager yet anxious to serve up the food I had spent the afternoon preparing, I thought again of my morning with Sean. Why did he discompose me so? Why should I be so taken up with him? How trivial indeed were my feelings when compared to my sister's illness, or my father's on-going grief over the untimely loss of his wife.

My thoughts ran on in their unruly way whilst Father and Mr. Cohen talked, and I carried the meal to table. I glanced at my violin, which was once more resting in its place inside the breakfront. The cabinet, brought with us from London, was a fitting home for it. Very finely wrought and decorated with cast bronze acanthus leaves, it was the best piece of furniture we possessed, and seemed far too grand for this family or house. It belied the fact that I had become little more than a servant girl, polishing it day in and day out whilst trying to wrench a moment from the light to practice my instrument. Even this morning, when all was said and done, I had not managed to play. Thus I was brought back by my meandering circle of thought to Sean, to his gleaming black hair, and to the easy charm which so improperly—yes, I was aware of that—so wrongfully bedazzled me.

"Rebecca," roared Father, gesturing to the contents of a bowl I was setting on the table, "What in the blessed name of God is this?"

"Indian corn, Father. It was all I could obtain."

"In Poland," he said slowly, his anger building, "they feed this to the pigs."

"Here many would count themselves lucky to get it," I replied boldly. "As you should be." I sat down at the table and commenced to eat.

"I should count myself luckier if I hadn't paid a full shilling and tuppence for it, my girl. Where did the money go?"

"Now, now, Mordechai," broke in Mr. Cohen, his fat little face trembling with good will and anxiety, his spectacles dancing on his nose. "This is a fine meal, a very fine meal, indeed. They do say that food costs very dear this autumn, on account of the blight."

Father sat back from his plate and folded his arms. "I want to know what happened to the money I gave you, Rebecca, and shall not rest until I hear."

"Mordechai, I beg of you..." quivered Mr. Cohen.

"Now!" shouted my father, face reddening, hands gripping his napkin.

"There was a family, a poor family that looked starved to the marrow, and I gave them half the money this morning, before I reached the shops."

"What?"

"I was thinking how fragile life is, Father. It could have been us just as well." I got up and walked back to the stove to fetch the kettle. Pouring hot water into the teapot, I returned once more to remove our much-prized Derby cups and saucers from the breakfront and lay them on the table. They were quite lovely, but their rich colours were like an insult to the poverty around us. "I do not see how we go on this way when there are people dying on the streets," I said at last.

"So you see, it was a blessing, Mordechai. The girl performed a *mitzvah*," interjected Mr. Cohen, shaking frightfully. A poor peacemaker indeed, he was clearly out of his depth in the choppy seas of our household.

"She did me no mitzvah, Shmuel. My daughter, my own daughter, has stolen the bread from our mouths." Father's anger was rising like a tide, whilst I awaited the inevitable wave of violence that I knew would be not in the slightest degree tempered by the presence of a guest. Suddenly his hand slammed viciously across the table, knocking one of our precious cups and saucers to the floor. There was a resounding crash as tiny shards of red, gold, and blue porcelain exploded across the room. Then there was silence, as I dragged my eyes away from the damage and the two of us confronted each other once more.

"There's herring in the cupboard, Tata, if you do not wish corn," whispered a tiny placating voice, and Father and I broke off our disagreement to stare at my sister as though she had suddenly wakened from a hundred-year sleep.

"My Sarahle, my dear Sarahle, how are you?" asked Father, rushing to her side, all fragments of our quarrel forgotten. Tenderly he patted her hand and smoothed her fair hair as if she were still a small child.

"Well, Tata, quite well, thank you. Only I should like it quiet now." And quiet it was, as I swept up the broken porcelain and we finished our meal. Later in the evening Father and Mr. Cohen were to sympathize with each other about the state of their respective businesses, whilst I cleared the plates with Sarah and marvelled at her new-found sanity.

"I do not know how we can go on much longer," sighed Father, looking with distaste at the drying mess of Indian corn in the bowl. "The poor cannot afford to buy from me and the rich want no man to see their wealth. And to think I left England to come here because I believed I'd lack competition."

"And so you do, Mordechai. There is no other jeweller for miles around."

"The shop is bad enough, but I've sold nothing at the market in a quarter," Father went on, completely disregarding Mr. Cohen. "This Saturday will be our last there if things do not improve." He stopped for a moment before adding sharply, "It was a wretched mistake I made the day I decided to remove us to this God-forsaken place."

"There now, there now," soothed his friend, optimistic to the last. "Everything will come right in the end, Mordechai. You'll see." He turned to me then, calling me *meine kind* and beseeching me to play an old Yiddish melody on my violin. I willingly obliged, imagining as its melancholy notes swelled through the house that we were back in Poland and my mother lived once more.

5

We did not go to the market that Saturday, as Father had caught a feverish chill in spite of the unseasonable heat. However, he was quite recovered two weeks later. Despite the fact that the weather had turned desperately cold suddenly, the wind blowing bitterly from the northeast, he announced we would try our barrow one last time before winter set in. The house was full of smoke and steam and washing drying interminably on racks in front of the fire, as it froze hard when I hung it outside, so I was not sorry to escape for a while. I hooked up my boots and wound my woollen cloak tightly around me, and we trudged down the hill to the square once more.

Sean was not there, and Sarah, who seemed quite well now, had elected to stay at home and observe the Sabbath. An hour or so after our arrival, Father marched off to speak to Mr. Cohen, looking intensely gloomy at the marked absence of any customers. Spider Fingers immediately sauntered up to our barrow and began rifling through the goods as though he'd never done me any harm.

"How can you stand there so brazenly when you stole my bracelets," I shouted, enraged.

"I never did. It was Sean Woodlock so he'd have something t'hand back to you," he grinned, examining a pearl button.

"And why in Heaven's name would he do that?" I asked stupidly, on tenterhooks for fear Father would overhear.

"He wanted to make your acquaintance, Re-becc-ah. Full of the blarney is our Sean. Does that to all the young girls, don't you know? He's the mightiest flirt this side of the Irish Sea." And he whirled away, sniggering.

I was dismayed by his words, and fancied at first that he said these things only to shock me, or to avenge himself for having been discovered in petty thievery. Although I was beginning to have a great faith in Sean, a trust in his strength and a feeling that he would always be there when I needed him, Spider Fingers had opened a sore and sorry place in my heart. From time to time I worried at it during the day. What, after all, were Sean's motives in befriending me? It was hard to think of him as a villain, but he was, as the boy had said, an excessive flirt who lacked all decorum in his dealings with me. I had imagined in my innocence that he kept his compliments for me alone and was intensely flattered, though it was more likely, I realized now, that he distributed them freely.

And what did I know of him anyway? A boy I had met at the market and become acquainted with on my front doorstep? Poor and ragged and, as if that wasn't enough, Catholic, a member of the religious group which had taunted and tormented us through history. But even as I doubted him, my eyes sought him out among the stalls and baskets, hopeful for a glimpse of his dark eyes and sunbeam smile.

Sean was kind, I truly believed that, and loving, and smart, and gentle. How could he, in all conscience, do me any harm? And why would I believe Spider Fingers, who had already proved himself a thief? Or had he? Misgivings swirled around me as the first snowflakes began to blow in a silvery gale across the cobbles, chilling to the bone the few poor souls who had ventured out in the cold, or who, sadly, had nowhere else to go.

"What a useless exercise this is," I said to myself. "I must fetch Father and persuade him to return home. There will be no business this day."

Father, however, was loath to leave his conversation with Shmuel Cohen. It certainly appeared that they were discussing something of importance as they huddled against the driving snow, shouting their words into the wind and gesturing to each other. I resigned myself to wait and did manage to peddle a couple of ribbons to a poor sad-eyed man who desired to cheer his sister. He dragged behind him a bony cow that he no doubt wished to sell, and I had a hard time deciding which of them looked the more miserable.

Finally, though, Father and I were on our way, pushing our barrow with great difficulty over the slippery road. Halfway up the hill I stopped in horror. Propped against a church wall, fully exposed to the storm, was a little family: a destitute mother and her three tattered children. They sat so curiously quiet and still that they resembled the image on a daguerreotype—so frozen that the smallest looked as though his arm, held out to beg, would snap off if I dropped a penny in his cap. He gazed back at me without blinking. Then, I suddenly realized with terrible dismay that he, his mother and sisters were all dead, transformed into ice statues by the wintry elements.

I cried out to Father, but he responded merely, as he continued to push uphill, "What have they to do with us? We must take care of our own," though he looked at them with a disconcerted stare as he moved by. I thought that I noticed moisture in his eyes. But it might well have been the cold or melted snowflakes, glistening like tear stains under his lids. I began to pray then to myself, repeating the words of the *Shema* over and over in my mind with quick desperation, but my supplications failed me entirely, unable to fill the fearful emptiness in my heart. It was as if I had carried my faith with me like a glove or handkerchief until that moment, little understanding its significance. Now, when I really needed it, its comfort eluded me. How could I worship a God who brought such terrible suffering to humankind? Why did he, why should he, visit such vengeance on the pitiful and helpless?

I ran ahead, glad to reach home and slam the door against the terrifying spectacle I had just witnessed. Desperate to pull off all reminders of the outside, I tore at my bonnet and cloak as though they would suffocate me. In a few moments, I heard the drag of the barrow as Father pulled it through to the back yard. He sounded like an undertaker hauling a coffin. There was a pause, then he entered with his arms full of unsold merchandise, saying jovially, as though nothing had happened, "Light a candle, for pity's sake, Rebecca. It's dark as the grave in here. I don't know how your sister can read."

"Yes, Father." I set a candlestick upon the table and bent over the fire to ignite a spill.

"And I hope you put on enough *cholent* to cook last evening. Mr. Cohen will be joining us for dinner."

"Father, how can you think of company at a time like this?" I burst out, throwing the spill back into the fire. Sarah put down her Bible and looked on mildly. "And why must that man be always with us?"

"Because, if I'm not mistaken, daughter, there will soon be a wedding in this family."

I looked from him to Sarah with stunned disbelief. The two of them appeared as gleeful as two school children who had just contrived some astounding magical trick. Sarah stood up, ready to address me further on the subject, but as she opened her mouth to speak, I interrupted her angrily.

"You are both mad," I shouted. "In fact, entirely deluded if you think you can persuade me to marry that silly old man." I picked up my cloak, wrenched open the back door, and fled from the house.

But standing between the barrow and the privy as the snow fell down on me, I could think of nowhere to go. Shmuel Cohen was out of the question, and the Benaris would merely smile apologetically before returning me to Father. I felt betrayed, abandoned by my family. Suddenly the door opened behind me, the subtle glow of lamplight illuminating the snow, and Father called out my name. Without further thought I tied on my cloak, still sopping from my previous outing, and ran away.

6

The snow had not let up at all but was now mixed with icy pellets, stinging and harsh against my skin. Having received directions from another tenant at whose home I had enquired, I approached Sean's cabin with hesitation, unsure of my reception. Why had I stumbled here, my boots entirely sodden, my cloak useless with wet and weighing me down? It was a gross breach of propriety, of that I was sure. If Father found out he would be within his rights to disown me, or worse, sit *shiva*—say the prayers for the dead for me. But I was drawn to Sean as to a powerful magnet, and no imbalance of wealth or religion could lessen that attraction.

There was no door to his house, only a ragged curtain drawn across a hole. This presented my first problem: how could I announce my presence without knocking? Timidly, I "hallood" twice or thrice but was not heard within, the wind having a far stronger voice than I. Now I was flummoxed but, growing colder by the instant, I couldn't remain outside much longer. So at last, with great fearfulness, I lifted the rag and stepped in.

The interior was mean indeed, cavelike, with damp dripping from the walls. It smelt of dirt and sweat and mud. There was not a candle or cup visible, no furniture either save a low wooden platform covered with straw, which I could only suppose to be a bed. Three little girls, half-naked and shoeless but with colourful ribbons in their tangled hair, sat close to a miserable peat fire, the smoke of which rose through a hole in the roof. One of them, the youngest child, I believe, was coughing dreadfully.

Hunkered in a corner with several other youths, his waistcoat and neckerchief missing, his shirtsleeves rolled up past his thin elbows, was Sean. Turning slowly, his eyes registering dull shock, he glared at me for several seconds before scrambling to his feet and saying ferociously, his mouth twisted into a snarl: "You should not have come, Rebecca. Here is not for the likes of you."

They were all staring at me now, and Sean's friends—for what else could I imagine them to be from their presence in his home?—rose quickly and slipped by me into the freezing night.

"How could you give me the eggs, Sean? How could you give them to me when you are all starving?" I sobbed with hurt and humiliation, before lifting my skirts and running from the dreadful place.

I managed to reach the top of the hill outside his cabin, tripping and stumbling through the deep snow, before his hand grasped my shoulder and spun me around. It was so slippery that the two of us almost fell down together. Close as we were, I kept my head averted so that he could not see my tears. But he placed his other hand under my chin and tilted it towards him, saying quietly, "You have shamed me, Becca, shamed me by coming."

He turned me again so that he stood behind me and, pointing, stated without emotion: "This is our farm, from this hilltop down to the 'house', if that is what you wish to call it, and from that grey rock over on that side to the blasted tree on the other. Even in a good year 'tis not enough to keep body and soul together. In a bad it yields nothing. And this piece of land we rent from the middleman, who has it from the agent, who manages it for the great and mighty landlord who lives far away in England. So besides my family, there are these three others, and all their servants and clerks and lawyers, who are itching to hew their wealth from this small nugget of rocky soil. Do you wonder that it cannot support us?" Snowflakes glittered on his bare arm, falling like jewelled stars onto his shirt. He took my hand and led me back into the cabin.

"Those three young men were here with me to discuss a course of action. We have eaten the food we should have traded for rent, and now have nothing to give the middleman. I urged them against violence, but they say 'tis because my mother lives in his house, and so I am protected. Perhaps in a way they are right. But 'tis the landlord we want, Becca, not any of his minions, for 'tis on him the whole miserable scheme of renting the land rests. We should rise against him like Molly Maguire did before. But he is far off and untouchable and wouldn't know want and poverty were he to be thrown head first into them."

I was sitting next to him on the bed now, still holding his hand, unable to speak from pity. The three little girls looked at us curiously but stayed by the fire, their faces flushed by the meagre heat.

"I'm still so young, Becca. Till this autumn I thought to be invincible. I believed I would triumph over poverty and carve a life for myself and my family. But now, as they evict my neighbours one by one, throwing them without compassion into the first cheerless storms of winter, I tell you, honestly, I think we will not overcome this crisis. But enough...enough!" he cried suddenly, rising from the bed, taking a few energetic steps, then turning toward me once more. "I had not meant to speak of this to anyone, and especially not to you. 'Twas self-pity that got the better of me. I have treated you unforgivably from the first moment I set eyes on you this night. Why have you come here in such savage weather? Things must be more than desperate at home."

"Whatever the problem was is meaningless now, Sean." How could I speak of Father and Mr. Cohen at such a time? My words would only trivialize Sean's suffering.

But little by little he drew the story out of me. "I need to know, Becca. You must tell me or I shan't sleep sound." He smiled his glorious easy smile, and after much urging I told him everything.

"Mr. Cohen is a kind man, is he not? I know him from the market."

This was hardly the response I had hoped for. Why was he not as outraged as I? "He's an old man. I cannot marry him," I said defiantly to close the matter.

"Sure, he's only forty at top-end and could give you a secure life, free from hunger and deprivation."

"What?"

"The owner of a pawnshop can only do better as things turn worse."

Was Sean teasing me? Did he not feel the bond between us that prevented me caring for anyone else? Or was he truly what Spider Fingers had suggested: a mighty flirt, never content to restrict himself to one young woman? As if he'd heard my thoughts, Sean continued gently, "I'd wed you myself, Becca, if I had any hope of looking after you, and if I thought for one moment you'd turn Catholic." He hesitated, then, "Would you turn?" he asked suddenly, his eyes speculative.

"No." The word was so barely audible that he had to strain to hear it.

"Ah. I thought not and should never have asked, but the church would not allow it else. Though by all that's holy, we worship the same God."

As usual, we were tangled in a difficult knot that I could not hope to unravel. Had he asked for my hand? Had I declined him? The moment had slipped by so rapidly that I wasn't entirely certain what had occurred, and now he was speaking again: "In any case, life seems to have nothing but misery in store for me at the minute. I would not drag a dog down to this level." He gestured around him at the appalling hovel that was his home and kicked absently at the mud floor. "I want to know you're well-provided for, because then, in a sense, I can bear things as they are."

I wiped my eyes on the back of my hand and spoke with conviction: "You are giving up on life too easily, Sean. It's as if you think you'll die." I thought again of the little frozen beggar by the church, his arm held out beseechingly, but put the image resolutely from my mind. "We cannot believe in failure when we're young. Death is something that must not happen to us."

"I will survive, somehow, Becca, and keep my family alive, but I cannot promise more than that." He stood silently for a moment before turning to his sisters, chiding them gently for not making their acquaintance with me sooner. The three girls immediately gathered around, inspecting my soaking clothes with wonder, and holding their hands out to me shyly.

"This is Miss Rebecca, who was kind enough to send you the charming ribbons you wear in your hair," he told them.

They thanked me prettily and I took their hands, grateful to be admitted in this limited way into Sean's family. It was unthinkable that I should one day play a larger role, though I worried for them like a sister. Had I not been earlier informed to the contrary, I should have guessed Mary's age at eight or nine only, so tiny and frail she was. The younger two, Peggy and Bridget, looked so starved and ill that it grieved my heart to see them, and Bridget still coughed most dreadfully.

"Mary, look to the others a while; I will not be gone long," said her brother. There was a ghastly sadness to his smile as he slipped on his waistcoat and jacket and turned towards me. "Now, is it home you're wanting to go, or did you wish to spoil your reputation entirely by staying here by me th'night?"

7

The storm had abated at last. As we descended to the town we came upon a number of the homeless, their narrow faces hollowed by night. Hunched over wretched fires and braziers, slender bundles of rags collected round them, they watched us speechlessly as we pressed through the ankle-deep snow. Somewhere close by a pipe played softly.

"God protect them," said Sean, crossing himself. "The agent's men will move them on come morning."

"What can we do?"

"Nothing, Becca. Be still. They will go to the poorhouse, most like, or..." His voice drowned by a sudden gust of wind, he grasped my hand tightly as he guided me over a fallen tree branch and finally into the city.

Now we were almost home, I dreaded having to climb the single step into my house. As we approached, my fear grew, for I could see light blazing from every window. This was all the more unusual because Father was so frugal. I realized forlornly there was little chance of my slipping in and up to bed without commotion. Sean released me and stood by a lamppost, light playing against the brooding shadow of his face. "We will be friends," he remarked, his voice sombre. Was it a statement or a question?

"Yes, always," I replied, shivering violently with cold and fear. "I don't want to go in, Sean."

He took my hand once more, caressing my little gold ring. "Never fear, Becca, I will come and see you," he promised, rolling the band between his thumb and middle finger thoughtfully, "as soon as I can. One morning I'll be knocking at your door. In fact, sooner or later," he smiled wryly, "you'll be glad to see the back of Sean Woodlock."

"I doubt that most sincerely."

"May I escort you in?"

"On no account." I trembled at the consequences of Father catching me in Sean's company a second time.

He leaned further towards me and touched my hair fleetingly. "Then I must get back to my sisters," he said abruptly and was gone, leaving only the casual imprint of his footsteps in the snow. I marvelled at how poorly I understood his intentions and my own. In the few novels I had read the heroine always read the hero's meaning most convincingly and charted her life as by the stars. I had entertained hopes that my life would follow the same comforting path. But, of course, I was no heroine. And Sean was not the right hero for me, not in the world's eyes, anyway.

I looked again at the house. What should I do now? Afraid to enter, I lingered on the road, but the front door opened almost immediately, Father climbing down the step with a lantern. "I thought I heard voices," he frowned to someone in the house, before calling out, "Rebecca, are you there?" Taking several steps forward into the snow, he shone the lantern back and forth. "In the name of God, daughter, answer me if you can."

Reluctantly, I stepped into the circle of light. "Here I am, Father."

He stood staring at me for a moment, anger, fear and relief mingling in the stern set of his features. Finally, as I had expected, rage took hold, and for a moment I was terrified that he was about to strike me. "With whom have you been?" he cried.

"What friends do I have to be with?" I replied, doing my best to look directly at him. "I have been wandering outside the town, trying to decide what to do."

My answer apparently satisfied him. With a shuddering sigh he regained his composure, saying, at last, with much difficulty: "Come along out of the cold, Rebecca. We have been worried to death at your disappearance."

He did not touch me but led the way in, and I followed fearfully. Candles burned everywhere, a dreadful extravagance, and dishes of food sat untouched on the table. It was incredible to look at such waste after the scenes of poverty outside, although I realized that the family's poor appetite was on my account. "Did you not want your dinner?" I asked, noticing with peculiar attention that Sarah had not done a good job of either laying the cutlery or setting out condiments.

"*Meine kind, meine kind,*" cried Mr. Cohen, rushing forward with such quivering intensity that he almost knocked me into Father's davenport, "we have been looking for you everywhere. I came for the lighting of the *Havdala* candle, as well as to dinner to celebrate our happy occasion, and found the house in an uproar."

I moved away from him as rapidly as possible, appalled afresh that he had requested my hand. I was tormented at the thought he might try to lay hold of me, although this was, of course, strictly forbidden by our religion. Sarah tiptoed over quietly, embracing me and inviting me to sit beside her at the table. As I did so, she confided, "It is I who am betrothed to Shmuel Cohen, Becky, not you. You quite mistook the matter earlier."

"You?" I looked at her with shock and bewilderment.

"Yes. He wishes to marry me." And here she beamed at the gentleman in question who, clearly having not the slightest notion of our subject matter, beamed back.

"But Sarah..." I whispered.

"Both he and Tata believe marriage will have a steadying effect on my character. And truthfully, I long for a family of my own." She sounded entirely rational as she spoke to me. This was always the crux of the problem with my sister. When in her correct mind, she appeared so right-headed and reasonable that it was close to impossible to imagine her otherwise. I saw at once that Mr. Cohen had fallen into this trap but doubted for not one moment that he would be disappointed. I knew from much experience that Sarah's sanity was an illusion.

While immensely relieved for myself, I was horrified that Father would allow this farce of a wedding to come about. He was merely passing his own problems on to someone even less capable of dealing with them, though now I thought on it, the entire arrangement made perfect sense from his perspective. How could I have thought Father wished me to marry Mr. Cohen? He would never have let me leave the house with Sarah still on his hands and nobody to look after her.

"Pray take off your cloak, *meine kind*," said Mr. Cohen kindly. "You are soaked to the skin. I cannot imagine why you would go wandering on such a treacherous night." He busied himself around me, removing the wet garment and hanging it over a chair. Father had not told him, then, the reason for my hasty disappearance. "Perhaps Sarah could furnish you with a hot drink," he continued.

"I will take one for myself, thank you, sir." I turned from him, eager to speak to Father before the betrothal went any further.

"Not now, Rebecca," he replied in response to my enquiry. He had no doubt sensed the content of Sarah's discussion with me and wished to avoid talking about it at all costs.

"I need to speak to you," I repeated, more urgently.

"Not now, Rebecca, I said. There will be time enough for talk in the morning."

"Allow me to prepare you a revitalizing drink myself, then, *meine kind*," interjected Mr. Cohen, so persistent in his courtesy that he had actually walked to the stove to fetch the kettle and was in grave danger of burning himself.

"Do not worry yourself on my daughter's account, Shmuel. She is more than capable of getting anything she wants," said my father sarcastically, taking the kettle from Mr. Cohen's hand and placing it on the hob by the fire. He then wished Mr. Cohen a hearty and unexpected good night, giving the bemused yet happy man his coat and ushering him as far as the front door. In return he was thanked quite enough times to last him a twelvemonth. Blowing out all the candles save one, Father grasped the last taper and climbed the stairs heavily to bed, leaving Sarah and me, as usual, in the dark.

8

My pleas to Father fell on deaf ears, as I had expected. The plans for the marriage continued apace, until one Wednesday, more than a fortnight later, when I was banking the fire against the cold. As he unwound the leather thongs of his phylacteries from his forehead and arm, Father informed me he would be taking Sarah with him that morning to witness the signing of the betrothal agreement.

"Then she is promised, and what is done cannot be undone." He rewound the *tefillin*, placing them in a little blue bag embroidered with a Star of David, as he did each forenoon. "And I wish to hear no argument from you, Rebecca. You have hampered me quite enough in the matter. First you say you should not marry Mr. Cohen, and then you insist Sarah should not."

"Nevertheless, Father, I beg you to reconsider. A betrothal agreement, as you say, is entirely irreversible. You do neither Mr. Cohen nor my sister a favour by..." He cut me off without ceremony, walking to the base of the stairs and calling up to Sarah to make haste, as he had not the entire day to spend on such matters. As she descended he tied her cloak for her, and they were soon out of the front door, conversing as though departing for a celebration which, in a sense, I suppose they were.

I had not much time to reflect for the house was in a tip, and almost certainly they would return with Mr. Cohen. There was much to be accomplished during their absence if I were not to incur additional wrath from Father. He seemed of late always burning with rage in my presence. Running first up to the bedrooms to spill the night slops into a pail, then back down to pull on my boots, I opened the back door and ventured out.

The snow was practically knee deep, drifted onto the barrow and along the fences. The weather had been unusually foul for weeks. Halfway to the midden to empty the refuse, picking my way carefully over an icy pathway, I encountered Sean, who was endeavouring to free the back entry from a fresh fall of snow so that he could come in. When he failed to open the gate, he passed the bag he was carrying carefully into the yard and jumped over the fence. He stood immediately before me. I almost died of embarrassment.

"I was just waiting for your father to leave, Becca. Didn't I tell you I'd visit as soon as I could?" He picked up the bag again.

"That was weeks ago," I reproached him. "I had quite given up on you." I looked around for somewhere to put the offending bucket, although I knew it was much too late to hide its contents from him.

"Haven't I awaited the best, the most timely moment?" His eyes were merry at the sight of me, and no wonder. I must altogether have made a comical appearance. Meaning to scrub the house from top to bottom before my family returned, I wore an old shirt of Father's with no corsets beneath, an enormous apron, and down-at-heel, unhooked boots. My skirt and petticoats were tucked under, into my drawers, and as if that weren't enough, I had on a great white mobcap of Mrs. O'Brien's to keep the wretched hair from my face. Sean separated the bucket from my hand and set it down in the yard, whilst I hastily adjusted my skirt to cover my ankles. Then he sat on the snow-laden step and laughed so lustily I was amazed he didn't slap his knee. "It does my heart good to see you, Becca. You are a tonic in bad times."

Mortified, I strode into the house and tore off the mob cap. As I stood warming my hands by the fire, there came a sharp rap at the back door. "It's open, as you very well know," I called.

"Aye, but may I come in?"

"Do as you wish." I went to sit down at the table, and Sean joined me immediately, kneeling before me and tenderly drawing off my boots.

"I am sorry, but you did make quite a spectacle." He was still laughing.

"Perhaps you could remind me of it again," I said sharply. But Sean had suddenly turned his attention to the table, rising to sit beside me and regarding with an anguished expression the scant remains of breakfast.

"Would you care for some oatmeal?" I asked softly. "There's plenty more in the pot."

"I could not eat while the girls sit hungry at home."

"Don't worry, I have something put by for them also. I was waiting for you to come so I could give it you."

If the intention was kind, Sean did not see it that way. He favoured me with a long, haughty stare and said only, "We have no need of your charity, Miss."

"I know, and you'd die rather than take money from me. You're a proud man, Sean Woodlock, but I thought we were past such foolishness," I replied, deeply offended. "Besides, it is customary to offer refreshment to guests." I went over to the stove, fetched the pot, and scraped the sticky porridge into a bowl. Then I banged it down before him. "The food is here for you. Take it or leave it."

I busied myself about the room, making tea, pouring it into mugs, buttering bread and setting it on the table. In fact, I did everything I could to prevent my seeing whether he ate or not but finally ran out of chores. I sat down with him again and lifted my drink. Keeping my eyes always on the rim of the mug, I sensed rather than saw the food was gone. Neither of us alluded further to the matter but languished in uncomfortable silence for several minutes.

"What have you brought with you?" I asked at last as I cleared the dishes and put them in a bowl to soak. I nodded towards the bag he had carried in.

"Uillean pipes, Becca." He seemed delighted to talk of something else. "New-fangled things, my daddy called them. But they sound like angels' voices at the very door of Heaven. There is nothing like them in all the world. I am playing at a tavern this night to try to prise some pennies free of their owners, so I brought them along."

"Might I not listen to them now?" I continued, pleased to have turned the conversation in so happy a fashion. Obligingly, he took them from the bag. Putting the small bellows of the instrument under his elbow, he commenced to play a haunting melody so intensely beautiful that for me it encompassed the proud and moody spirit of Ireland.

Comprehending at once that I was entirely captured by the music, he begged me to take out my violin so he could teach me that tune and another, a fast jig, which he mentioned he had composed himself. We practised the latter for some time. Then, almost of one accord, we put down our instruments and began to dance, I in my bare feet, he in his boots, galloping around downstairs like a pair of children and laughing all the while. After several minutes he collapsed into a chair, pulling me down on his knee.

"Now if anyone asked me where I had been this morning, and I said to the house of a lovely auburn-haired girl, and they asked me what I did, and I answered I played the pipes while she played the fiddle, and then we both danced like the devil, they would take me for a complete eedjut, Becca. But this is the finest time I have had since these bad days began," he said, nuzzling my hair. I stood up immediately and moved swiftly away from him. How stupid I was to have invited him into the empty house with me. I blushed with shame. Suddenly brought to my senses and stone cold with worry, I realized that Father might return at any minute.

"If I had wished to take advantage of you, I could have done so months ago," Sean said stiffly, standing also. "At my home, or up in the hills."

"I beg your pardon, Sean, but in my religion it is forbidden for a young man to dance with a young woman, or even to touch her hand without a kerchief between them." I thought with terrible regret and nostalgia of our last meeting, recalling how we had held fast to each other when I feared the famine would overwhelm him. "I should have told you sooner. We have both got carried away, I suppose."

"I would never hurt you, Becca. I've said it before. I just don't know your ways."

"Sean, you should go now. I'm afraid Father will find you here."

"Would that be so terrible?" he asked sadly. Crestfallen, he took up his pipes, stowing them carefully in the bag before moving towards the door.

Ashamed of having treated him so badly, yet unable to find words capable of easing the situation, I hurried instead to make up a small parcel of provisions. Although not buying more of late, I was deliberately eating less so a saving was made, and Father did not notice any difference in the bills. Truth to tell, the shops were choked with food now, if one but had the money to purchase it.

"This is for the girls," I said, "And you also if you have a mind. I'm sorry it cannot be more." He began to protest, but I said only, "If you had and I had not, would you allow me to starve?"

"Becca, Becca," he replied, looking at the floor.

"I do not know what else to do, Sean, how else to help. People are dropping on the streets; death has become a commonplace. And all I have is this miserable package of eggs and bread to give. Please oblige me by taking it."

"You are my respite," was all he said, but this time he accepted.

I held my hand out to him as he left, and he hesitated for an instant before touching my fingers guardedly. He looked ready to say something, then seemingly changed his mind. But he turned to me one last time, speaking in low tones. "I passed this way the other night, and there was a row of little candles on the sill, their tiny flames striving toward the glass. It seemed to me then that each candle expressed some shimmering aspect of you, your charm, your warmth, your soul. And I wanted all morning to say that I think we share the same faith, Becca, under the differing mantles of our religions."

"Those candles were to celebrate *Chanukah*, our Festival of Light," I replied softly, "when oil enough for one night burned for eight. If only that could happen with food, so there'd always be enough to eat."

"'Tis said in the Bible that our Lord multiplied the number of loaves and fishes to feed all who gathered to hear him."

"Well I wish he'd do it again. Watching people starve has destroyed my faith."

"I am so sorry, Becca, because knowing you has restored mine."

I was much taken by what he had said and could not continue for a moment. "Sean," I added at last, just before closing the back door, "there is something of great importance I have been wishing to tell you also. I am not betrothed to Mr. Cohen after all. He is to marry my sister." Greatly comforted by his parting expression, I went back and sat at the table, taking ease in the fact we had not been discovered. It was not long, however, before I grew unsettled again and jumped to my feet. I would have to hurry if I were to sweep the floor and prepare a meal before Father, Sarah, and my future brother-in-law returned.

9

All the while Sean was at the house, I hid from him a plan I had devised earlier to relieve his family's plight. Although not well versed in the rituals of Christmas, I knew it was traditional to give small presents, much as we distributed *gelt*, or money, at Chanukah. Doubting heartily Sean's sisters would receive even a decent meal that day and desperate to find a way to ease my mind of the tremendous guilt I felt at always having enough to eat, I worked whenever Father was away at providing a small surprise for them. Accordingly, I had cast about amongst my possessions until I came upon a grey shawl of the softest wool. Unravelling it little by little, I tied broken ends together and knitted mittens for the three girls and a muffler for Sean. When I had completed my task I made warm socks also, recalling the children's frozen feet and the miserable fire at their home.

"What are you doing?" asked Sarah one day, looking up from her reading of the Bible.

I was struggling with a dropped stitch and took a moment or

two to reply. "Knitting for the poor," I said at last. This was not totally inaccurate. On the whole, I preferred not to tell untruths.

"Could I do that, too?"

"With pleasure." I furnished her with needles and yarn, but she finished only half a sock before returning to her reading.

The days passed quickly with this new diversion to occupy my time. I also hoarded little packages of flour, sugar, and corn, as well as a small cheese and some biscuits I had recently baked. As the holiday drew closer I made up a basket of both the food and gifts to fetch to Sean's, thinking only of the joyous expressions of unexpected pleasure my gift would cause. I little thought Sean would refuse me this time. We had come too far for that.

But in spite of my confidence, there still seemed something missing. After a small struggle with myself I added my peg doll as a present for the smallest child, Bridget, taking my old baby from the bed and smoothing her clothes out wistfully before tucking her in with the other surprises. Mr. Cohen had given me a sovereign for Chanukah and, with no regret, I dropped this also into the basket.

I was expecting to go up on Christmas Eve, but on the twenty-third, whilst we were at our evening meal, a timid knock sounded at the back door. Surely this could not be Sean. He would know better than to visit when the family was home. But before I could take a step, Father had already risen and was making his way through the scullery. "I'll see to this. Get on with your dinners," he said. But how could I concentrate on my food when I had no idea who stood at the door?

Father was soon back. "It was only a poor peasant girl, begging no doubt. These people think I'm made of money and have nothing better to do than cater to their wants." He took up his knife and fork and began eating again, pushing a large piece of salted beef into his mouth.

"Well, I must give her something," I retorted, getting up and grabbing a heel of bread from the table. "We cannot turn her away entirely in such wretched weather."

Ignoring my father's objections, I hastened through the scullery and threw open the door. Imagine my astonishment at finding Sean's eldest sister on the step. She stood shivering and barefoot in the snow, clearly uncertain as to whether she should stay or leave. "Please, Miss Rebecca," she whispered as soon as she set eyes on me, "you're to come up as soon as you can." The child had clearly been crying.

"Why, what is it, Mary?" I asked, stricken. But she was already gone, running across the yard and up the laneway. If I wanted to discover what was the matter, I would have to find out for myself.

I hid the bread in my pocket and returned to my meal, my pulse hammering uncontrollably. Unable to eat, I sat mute. What could be so wrong that Sean would ask for me? Could he be ill? In some wretched trouble? Should I risk everything by going up tonight, or wait till the morrow? Father's voice, loud and demanding, cut through my thoughts: "Well, daughter? Well? Well?"

"I beg your pardon, Father?"

"Well? Did you find my description of the scene inadequate?"

"Oh...no, it was quite as you said. A poor peasant girl. I gave her the piece of bread."

He drew his chair close, thrusting his reddened face into mine. "If you take one step, one step mark me, out of line, you will answer to me. Is that understood?"

"Perfectly, Father." He was growing suspicious. I would go up tomorrow.

10

"I will open the shop today, though Heaven knows there has been little enough trade of late. God willing, someone will wish to pick up a trinket for the Gentile holiday." Father pulled out his fob watch, snapped it open, and checked the hour. Replacing it in his pocket and reaching for his hat and coat, he said only, "I will return at six," before quitting the house.

"I am going shopping, Sarah," I told my sister as I replaced the teapot in the breakfront and closed the doors. "There is little enough in the house for dinner."

"But your basket is already full, Becky. How can that be?"

"I have here all the socks and mittens I knitted for the poor, and will distribute them on the way."

The explanation seemed to appease her, and she settled back in her seat. As I was going out the door, however, she called out: "But you have no money, Sister. Father left you not a penny."

"I have my Chanukah gelt. Father can repay me later." I lifted the latch, itching to be gone. But a blizzard was blowing outside, and I wondered greatly why Father had left at all. It had not looked half as bad through the window, but now that I was in the midst of it I was thoroughly afraid I would be blown away. Burdened by the basket, which despite its poor contents I clutched as tightly to me as a treasure chest, I could not keep my cloak about me properly. It blew like a ship's sail in my wake, scarcely affording me any warmth or protection. My hood had blown off, too, and I hung onto my bonnet with my free hand, lest it should be swept across the countryside by an even heavier gust.

The snow was falling so heavily I could hardly see a yard in front of my face, and I was worried that I might pass Sean's home and go off in the wrong direction. Trees and bushes loomed out of the storm like ice-bound spirits; branches caught at my clothing as I passed. I turned and turned again and at the summit of a hill stopped and stared around me, half blind, frantic and lost. Then a voice called above the gale: "Hello, Re-becc-ah. Looking for our Sean's, are you? You have quite missed the spot. And so much happening there today."

It was Spider Fingers. I felt a surge of disgust as he emerged from the veil of snow, loath to understand how he might have found me. "You've been following me," I accused him.

"Not so, not so, Re-becc-ah. I ran into you by chance."

"Well, now you can go away."

"In this weather? That would hardly be gentlemanly," he grinned. "And besides, you look as panicked as a bee trapped in a jar. Just follow me, and I'll have you to the place in five minutes." I hesitated, unwilling to have anything to do with him, but in the end relented. I had little chance of finding Sean's home on my own, with the thick wintry blanket concealing all. Amazingly, Spider Fingers was for once as good as his word, though I could not help but wonder at his motives.

He led me there quickly, then departed with exaggerated

courtesy, and I lingered in the cold, frightened at what I might find within. How did the loathsome creature know I was going to Sean's? What had he meant about so much happening there today, and why had I not asked when I had the chance? But as I waited for a little courage to infuse my veins, I heard the poignant music of the pipes, almost heartbreaking, issuing from the interior. Drawn irresistibly by the mournful sound, I breathed deeply and lifted the ragged curtain. I could only wish then that I had never entered.

The bed, the cabin's sole item of furniture, had been cleared of straw and on it lay a corpse swathed in a white sheet. Three candles were placed at the head. Mary, Bridget, and Peggy were all kneeling close by, sobbing, and a woman I had never seen before, gnarled and dressed in black, rose and began to keen in Irish as soon as she saw me. Her dark eyes were glittering, her hands raised high in the small room. There were others present, too, but I sought out only Sean, terrified for a moment that his might be the body lying ready for burial.

But he must have seen me first, for he stood up and came to me instantly. My heart was so eased by the sight of him I dropped my basket. As he stretched out his arms I moved into them willingly, wet and frozen as I was, resting my head against his chest.

"Who, Sean, who?" I whispered.

"My mam," he said simply, as he untied the ribbons of my bonnet. "They were gunning for the middleman, but she stood in their way."

I wanted to comfort him, but his body tensed and he thrust me aside. Looking up, bewildered at how I might have offended him, I saw that he was not angry at me but glared steadily at the entrance. One of the youths from my first visit stood there, his eyes wild, dark hair streaming in the gale. "I'm sorry, Sean," he cried. "It was nothing to do with me, I swear to God."

Sean took a step forward and grabbed the hapless boy by the collar. "Get out, James Ryan, out of my house. Get out of the country if you know what's good for you. My mam's dead, and her blood is on your hands. She was a good woman, who never did anyone any harm. I swear I'll kill you if I ever set eyes on you again." He shoved Ryan violently from him, and the boy tripped, pitching into the wall. He gave a long moan and lay still.

"Come away, Sean. Come away now," murmured an older man, seizing him by both arms and holding him close. After a moment, Ryan scrambled up and looked round groggily. Then he vanished into the storm.

"By all that's holy, Becca," declared Sean, returning to me a little later when he had composed himself, "I don't even know which side I'm on any more."

That afternoon Sean's mother was buried in a cairn, the earth too glacial to take her. Each neighbour had brought a rock, and these they placed around her as the snow bloomed over her shroud. How cold it was—death weather. Shivering, I thought again and again of the concealed woman, her life stopped up in ice and stone. She was Sean's nearest relative, and he had loved her dearly, yet now I would never have the chance to meet her.

As night fell, the storm raged across the moon. A priest came up from the parish to say a prayer over her grave, his Latin lost in the gale as the torches swayed and doused. I had only witnessed Hebrew services before and slipped to the back, feeling odd and out of place. The people stared at me but said nothing, no doubt in deference to Sean, though they recognized me for an outsider, someone who did not have to suffer their appalling misfortunes this miserable winter. I did not know them, would never have to answer to them. Why then did I feel so uncomfortable?

Afterwards, I was anxious to go, more particularly as I thought of the argument awaiting me at home. I could almost sense Father bloating with rage as my absence continued. But how could I leave Sean after such a tragedy? He had sought me out, and now I must stay by him.

It was only after the mourners had departed, late into the evening, that Sean made preparation to take me back to my house. Although I objected, saying he must abide by his family, he was adamant.

"Sure, Becca, and I'm going to let you go down by yourself in this squall. Wasn't it bad enough to let you come up on your own? But I craved your company so badly at this time, I didn't know what else to do."

"Have you informed your Father of the loss, Sean?"

"I haven't heard from him these two years and don't even know if he's alive or dead. My daddy's never been much of a one for responsibility, anyway. It's only me left now to look after the three little ones, and how I'm going to manage I cannot say."

"Surely the middleman will forgive you the rent, after what happened."

"He's dead also, Becca. Did I not tell you? The bastards didn't stop at one. And now the whole intrigue has backfired on them, for the rent reverts to the landlord, I should think, and he's never been known to show an ounce of pity, nor his agent neither." He stopped for a moment to pull on his cap and jacket, plunging his fingers deep into the pockets as though hunting for coins. "All we had was my Mam's wages, two pounds of the eight needed to pay, but I've spent that on the wake. I know I might not have, but I couldn't feel right about sending her to her grave with nothing to mark her passing." He was crying. I put up my hand to wipe the tears from his eyes. He grasped it at once, too proud to admit his frailty, and we plunged out into the blizzard.

We were soon in the thick of it, the storm blasting down upon us. Snow fell into our eyes and mouths, isolating us from each other, and it wasn't until we reached the back step of my house that I spoke. There was a memory I had never mentioned to anyone, that I had held painfully to myself throughout my childhood, but which I now needed to share with him, even though I knew it might injure both of us.

"Sean, my mother was killed, too. She was dragged out of the house while we played. I was very tiny then and hid under the bed, but my sister Sarah ran out after her and saw everything." I took out the miniature and showed him Mama's likeness, saying I would certainly give the portrait to my own daughter, if I ever had one.

"Who killed her?" he asked, his voice grim.

"Christians," I replied, not knowing how to diminish the hurt. "It was Easter. That's why Father moved us from Poland. He thought we would be safer."

11

The house was dark as I slipped through the back entrance, only the remains of the last Chanukah candles throwing out a tiny encircling light. Perhaps Father had gone to bed after all. Reduced to embers, the fire glowed feebly in the grate, providing little warmth, whilst the long case clock ticked in the hall, loud in the evening's calm. Halfway across the room I started, as with a sudden whoosh an oil lamp flamed upwards, its aura revealing Father's face. He had been sitting in his armchair by the fireplace all along, waiting to pounce like a cat on a mouse.

"Come here, Rebecca," he said, standing up and elongating the vowels of my name until they sounded almost as though they had been spoken by Spider Fingers.

"No, Father," I replied, knowing too well the punishment that awaited me. I removed my bonnet and set it on the table with elaborate care, wishing to delay the inevitable.

"Come here, I say, or I shall come to you."

I moved in his direction slowly, my legs heavy as lead,

stopping short of him in order to protect myself with my arm. But he took a single step towards me, crying out only: "You are a disgrace to this family." There was a terrible pause. Then he pulled my arm away and struck me savagely on the face. I grabbed hold of a chair to prevent myself from going down.

"What right have you to touch me? I have done nothing wrong," I whispered.

Enraged by my opposition, he hit me again, and this time I fell hard against the table. The wet bonnet cushioned my arm somewhat, though a candlestick crashed to the floor. I could hear Sarah rushing down the stairs. The clock struck the quarter, and I wondered how late it was. Ten? Eleven? What mattered it anyway?

"You were seen...holding hands with a Gentile...going to his house. You know very well it is forbidden for any man to touch you, but this...this is an outrage."

"It is forbidden also to sell at the market on the Sabbath, but we do it all the time."

"Are you mad? Can you not tell the difference?" He raised his hand a third time, but Sarah stepped between us, catching hold of his arm whilst begging him earnestly to desist. He pulled away in disgust.

"Father," I sobbed, "please. I feel in my heart I have committed no crime, done nothing of which I should be ashamed. I went to Sean's house today for his mother's funeral." I sat down on a chair, wiping my eyes on my sleeve. My cloak, still sodden from the storm, weighed me down like ballast.

Father bent over me, his shadow immense in the lamp-lit room. He was eyeing me with such repugnance I wanted to die. "Sean is it? Sean? Sean? I will hear nothing further. Nothing, do you understand? And if you ever speak to this boy again, speak, mark you, not anything more than that, I will act on information given to me and go straight to the authorities."

I looked up at him with stunned disbelief. What in Heaven's name could he be talking about? "What information? Sean has not committed any crime. Nor could he. He is the kindest, the most gentle..." But a memory of him pushing Ryan violently across the room came unbidden to my mind.

"In my opinion, the greatest crime he committed was to form a liaison with you. For that I will never forgive him. The constabulary, however, would be more interested to know that he killed his own mother whilst trying to murder the person to whom he owed rent."

"What? That's not true. Who would tell such an awful lie?"

"Whether a lie or no," replied Father, neatly sidestepping my question, his words oozing like venom into the cold air, "I'm certain the authorities would be glad to hear of it. Do you understand?"

I nodded mutely.

"You shall never speak to him again." He took my silence as acceptance. "And from now on you will not leave this house without an escort. Sarah will accompany you." This was the cruellest thrust of all. For so many years I had guarded my sister, keeping her out of harm's way. Now, in a bizarre and puzzling reversal, she was assigned to watching me.

"Go to your bed now, before I lose control altogether and throw you out into the storm." Father settled back by the fireplace and, turning away from me, dropped his head in his hands. He started to make a dry, hard, choking sound as though sobbing. I went upstairs with Sarah, nursing my bruised face and wondering who could have been so ruthless, so filled with hate, as to visit him this day and tell him such a monstrous concoction of truth and fiction.

12

There were two people, I realized, who could have told Father: James Ryan and Spider Fingers. Ryan may have had motive but had hardly made my acquaintance. Spider Fingers knew me, yet as far as I could make out had no motive other than his spiteful nature. I put the horrid business out of my mind at last, for there was no solution to it.

The memory of Father's crying, however, was far more distressing. "He is doing what he thinks best," said Sarah in her quiet voice, as I climbed into bed that night. "He likes it no more than you do." She was in all likelihood correct. Surprisingly, my sister sometimes exhibited a good deal of common sense, particularly in her calmer moments.

"But he cuts me off from my life," I complained, as I slipped under the coverlet.

"Your life is here with us, Becky, and you'll know it well enough if you'll only consider and stop obliging Father to remain so angry with you."

I shifted away from her but could not sleep, remembering again the horrible sound of Father sobbing. The last time I had witnessed him crying was on the occasion of my mother's funeral. Sean had wept also this day, although he, like Father, was ashamed for me to see him do so. It was hard, hard, to see men weep. I could not help but feel a tremendous love and pity for both of them, although in Father's case my emotions were mixed with a profound confusion and anger.

There was a deadness inside of me like a flame extinguished. Friends, Sean had called us, and I hoped we should always be; he was my one true ally, and I did not know how I might manage without his warmth and understanding. I was distraught at the idea of foregoing his company altogether and spent many an hour locked in battle with myself over the consequences of such a move. In the end I decided the alternative was the more dreadful; I must abide by Father's will and separate myself from Sean, for the present at least. That way he would be safe from arrest, and his sisters would keep their provider. Although, had I earlier dreamed it? I imagined him, as I went about my chores, flung deep into the bottom of a pit, like Joseph of the twelve tribes, with only myself possessing the power to recover him.

Two days later, as I fought my way back from the privy in the deep snow, I noticed my basket sitting by the back door. With the stormy events of the wake I had forgotten it completely. The basket was now empty, as I would have wished, save for a tiny article wrapped in newspaper. This paper, torn from The National, had the words "Thank you" scrawled across it. I hurriedly unwrapped it, hoping Sean had not been so impulsive as to buy me a gift. But inside, winking up at me, was my sovereign. "Why the stupid, stubborn idiot," I cried, kicking the basket into the yard. "His pride will kill him one of these days."

How slowly the weeks passed. The snow continued to fall, and it was rumoured that in some parts of the country the drifts were so deep they covered the tops of houses. A virtual prisoner, I ventured out only rarely, and then with Father or Sarah as my guardian. Once at dusk I thought I saw Sean lounging against a lamppost in the sleet, his collar drawn up and his hands in his pockets. When I looked again he was gone, and I realized it was likely only my imagination playing tricks on me. Most days, though, there were no such distractions, as I completed the housework, cooked, and practised the violin when I had a moment or two to spare. In effect, life had returned to its old narrowness, with the difference that I now knew something was missing.

Father had engaged a dressmaker to sew Sarah's wedding gown, but for the rest of her trousseau, my sister and I were responsible. We set to work diligently to seam sheets and bolster cases, petticoats and drawers. Or rather, I set to work whilst Sarah, who was becoming more restless by the day, flitted around the room chattering in a high excited voice.

"When I am married you shall come and visit me, Becky. Perhaps you will be married too."

"I highly doubt that."

"Well then, perhaps I shall have a servant," she continued, spinning round and curtsying to the inkwell on the davenport.

"That is the more likely, I believe," I replied, holding a piece of hemming to the light to assure myself it was straight.

"They do say Mr. Cohen is rich, although we will not have any dishes as good as the Derby. Are you sure that is the best lace for those petticoats? The seamstress says there is a dearer, prettier kind at the haberdasher's. Also, I forgot to tell you, I will need a new dress for summer, besides the bridal gown. My other is quite worn out." On she prattled, scarcely taking any notice of my responses, if at any time I had sufficient opportunity to make them. Sometimes I wondered, given her mounting excitement, whether the wedding would take place at all.

It was during a brief pause in her talk one day that we both heard a soft knock on the door. "That must be the woman come for a fitting of the dress," said Sarah, rushing away to admit her. A moment passed before I heard her say quite plainly, "My sister does not wish to know you, sir."

My pulse leapt and I moved to the entrance of the hall in time to hear Sean remark, very politely, "Please beg her to come out so she may answer for herself."

"That is impossible," replied Sarah, her voice shrill and agitated. "I pray you leave."

Too polite to walk unbidden into the house, too obstinate to go away, Sean stood on the step, as my sister, flustered, again beseeched him to depart. I walked out to him then, my knees almost buckling with fright. Pushing Sarah very gently aside, I said with much difficulty: "Please go away, Sir. I may not see you any more."

"I'm sorry, Becca, to come whilst family is here," he responded, his pinched face almost breaking my resolve, "'Tis not my way to compromise your position. But there is Black Fever in the town, and I needed to know you were well."

"I am quite well, thank you, but my father does not wish me to speak to you. So it would be better for all concerned if you would consent to leave."

I hoped against hope he would understand my message, and as he looked sideways for a moment, reflecting, I thought that he did; however, he straightened his stance, staring angrily into my eyes. I recognized the old arrogance reasserting itself. "So I'm not good enough for your acquaintance, is that it?"

"Yes, that appears to be it," I replied slowly, well aware Sarah would convey every word I uttered back to Father, if she could keep it in her brain long enough. "I sincerely hope your sisters are well. Good day to you, sir." And I shut the door, feeling my loss most acutely.

13

Mrs. O'Brien still came to the house to wash the linens, if we could only find place to hang them. She was, moreover, my best source of news. As she scrubbed Father's shirt collars one Monday whilst I rinsed and wiped the dishes, she told me, amongst her other bits of gossip, that a group of Protestant ladies had set up a soup kitchen not far from our house. I was very glad to hear this, though little understood her grimace as she said the word Protestant. Were these women not Christians like herself?

"In a manner of speaking, m'dear," she sniffed, sweating with effort. "But most good Catholics will not tolerate them, for they do not belong to the one true religion, d'you see?"

I didn't see at all. "Then of course I do not either?" I asked, putting down the dishcloth.

"That's different, Miss, for as we both well know, you are a heathen."

I should have been outraged but let her remark pass, dwelling instead, with great concentration, on the more important part of her communication: that people were trying at last to relieve the wretched conditions of the starving. Where was this place? Who was allowed to eat there? And who might help?

"One minute, one minute, please. Your questions rain so fast upon me I cannot get me words strung together. It's a Protestant kitchen, as I said, set up not a mile from here. The soup is for those poor who have tickets of entitlement. And I expect anyone who is not afraid of the fever can help. Though you would not want to go," she said hastily, suddenly understanding the enthusiasm in my voice. "You never know what you'll catch there. No, Miss Rebecca, it is not for the likes of you."

If I had heard these words before from another quarter, I liked them no better a second time. "You are probably right, Mrs. O," I said, not wishing to provoke her. I took up my cloth again to finish the dishes, gazing out of the high scullery window as I worked. The inside of the pane was caked with ice, as indeed were all the windows of the house. Outside, I glimpsed the pathway to the privy, a little distorted by the rime. Of necessity Father or I now shovelled it clear each day, as well as the snow-covered midden. A tiny robin splashed like crimson paint across the landscape, landing on the sill. Perhaps he was the first true herald of spring.

I was determined to talk to Father about the possibility of helping in the soup kitchen. His decision that my sister should accompany me everywhere had not prevailed for long. She was growing so moody and excitable again that I was having to watch after *her* to ensure she did not disappear barefooted into the snow. Although I supposed I could have done as I pleased in the matter, I wanted this time to be totally clear and above board so he could not later hold my secrecy against me.

"Father, please," I pleaded, after having received an absolute negative in response to my request. "I have felt so helpless these last months."

"Why must it always be an argument with you, Rebecca? My answer is no and will remain thus. Let that be an end to it."

"I will do as I wish," I informed him coldly. "You have cajoled, bullied, and beaten me in the past. With none of these methods will you ever triumph over me again, for I am absolutely resolved to do what I can to relieve the suffering. I will go on Mondays, when Mrs. O'Brien is here to keep an eye on Sarah. I promise you I will not seek out Sean, if that is what you are worried about, but if you do not like my going you will have to lock me out of the house."

He was eating his supper of herring and black bread. Although I waited for his response, a plate overturned in anger or his fist slammed down upon the table, mercifully neither circumstance occurred. However, a few minutes later he replied sharply, "You go too far, too far by half, Rebecca. And what if you get sick?"

"If I become sick, I shall not expect you to look after me."

"As if I could not," he said gloomily. Then, perhaps defeated for the once, he touched on the matter no more.

I set off for the soup kitchen early the next Monday, having received exact instructions as to its location from an extremely disagreeable Mrs. O'Brien. The house was in an easterly direction, and as I approached, the clouds blazed orange as the rising sun, still invisible, sent streamers of fire across the dark sky. As they faded to a rosy hue, tinting the ground, I noticed for the first time that the snow had slowly begun to recede, like a great tide departing the shore, pulling away from walls and fences and revealing a little green where the grass began to reclaim its territory. How could the world be so beautiful this dawn, so new and promising, when all around me people were struggling for their survival?

The house was large and of excellent proportions, situated in one of the best neighbourhoods of the town. Greeted at the door by a maid, and ushered in to meet a well-dressed lady by the name of Mrs. Andrews, I introduced myself and set forth my carefully rehearsed reasons for coming.

"But you are the daughter of the jeweller, are you not?" she replied, after having considered me carefully. "You are...you are...I don't know quite how to phrase it without appearing indelicate."

"A Jew?"

"Exactly." She was silent for a moment, as if poised at a crossroads. "My dear young lady," she said finally, smoothing her brown silk gown and declining to look at me further, "this is a Protestant undertaking and, I believe, if you will forgive my forthright opinion, that you will make everybody involved in it feel quite uncomfortable if you remain."

"Forgive me, Madam, but I understood you were here to help the starving." Seething with anger, I remained outwardly calm only with the most enormous effort. "What has discomfort to do with it?" I asked quietly. "Do I not also see the poor parade by my window every day? Am I not allowed to feel compassion too? And do you not need extra hands, no matter what religion God has assigned to them?"

A slow flush spread up Mrs. Andrews' face, stopping only at the silver roots of her hair. "You are quite right in what you say, my dear. I apologise most sincerely. It is for the Almighty to decide on His helpmates, not we wretched sinners. I see you have your apron on, so if you will come into the kitchen we will find something for those helpful hands of yours to do."

I went with her willingly and assisted her and the other ladies on that and other Mondays. The work, though similar to what I did at home, seemed less like drudgery, for I could see the good that sprang from it. I peeled vegetables, cooked and served soup to the great flood of starving beggars who surged through the back door and presented their tickets. Little by little the ladies warmed to me, treating me as one of themselves. There could be no doubt it was a wonderful program administered by caring and selfless women: it kept people alive. Yet it was also all but unbearable to look into the hunger-ravaged faces. After a time, as a kind of self-protection, I scarcely noticed who came or went.

One Monday in early March I was serving as usual. Thirty people must already have passed me in the line, their ancient jugs and bowls held up for the thick stir-about of Indian corn and rice, when the hand now extended wakened something intensely emotional in me. I looked up. A pair of dark, grey eyes glared back at me. "Condescending, Miss? Ministering to the poor?" Sean was smouldering with rage and shame. "So how does it feel to be playing the lady of the manor again?" His three sisters trailing him like hungry ducklings, he turned fiercely and walked away.

14

I had not seen him for almost two months and the changes in him were deplorable. Emaciated, tattered, barely able to support himself upright, he aroused in me a dreadful and relentless pity and self-reproach. No matter what the circumstances, no matter how dangerous, I should never have abandoned him. I could have managed something, anything, even if it were only to get word to him that I still considered him my friend. I had worried about him, missed him, each hour of every day, but had imagined him always as he was before. It had never occurred to me that such a brief passage of time could bring about this awful transformation. Only his pride remained intact.

"Is there anything amiss, Rebecca?" asked Mrs. Andrews, coming over from the far side of the room.

"No, thank you, Madam. But the youth I was speaking to is an acquaintance of mine, and I must see how he does."

She was far too civilized to say anything, though her eyes widened as I passed her my ladle. I ran outside, catching up with

Sean on the pathway. "If it please you, Sean," I begged, "return and take something to eat, if not for yourself then for the girls."

"I do not care for it; no more do they," he replied, shrugging off my arm. "Leave me go, Miss."

"You are wrong, wrong in what you think of me. I never meant to give up your friendship."

"Leave me go, I say. 'Tis no desire I have to throw you down, but I'd rather starve than stay here."

This last remark was so crushing I began to sob, grasping the torn material of his jacket as he pushed me away. "Please, please," I pleaded, "do not go. I could not bear it." I was almost to the wet gravel on my knees, heedless of the many who stood around staring at me. "Give me leave to explain. Understand."

He stood for a minute, uncertain. "Ah, Becca," he said, relenting then and drawing me up, "however did we come to this pass?" Shivering, I felt the sharp bones under his skin. He was close to starving.

"Come back inside, Sean. Eat and allow your sisters to eat. Afterwards we may talk." He needed little further persuasion and accepted the stir-about from the kitchen, feeding most of it to the girls, taking only the little left in the bottom of the container for himself. It was the kind of gesture I had long come to expect from him. I endeavoured to give him more, but he refused, saying he would take what was due to his family, and nothing extra.

After the food supply was exhausted and all the pots washed and put away for the day, Mrs. Andrews nodded for me to leave, and I went out to speak to him. The thaw was well underway, and the trees were budding despite the heavy residue of melting snow that still clung to the roads and byways. We stood in the yard of the house, gazing out at the countryside, the slight promise and scent of spring entirely welcome after the long winter.

The two older girls were sitting some way off along the wall. "'Tis almost St. Patrick's Day, and the fields are still locked under the ice," sighed Sean, who looked somewhat better after his scant meal. "But I have nothing to plant anyway, for we have eaten every blessed seed potato that we had, and the eyes afterward. What was it you wanted to tell me, Becca?"

"I am so sorry I turned you away from my house, Sean. Though it was solely to protect you, or I should never have done it." I needed no prompting but told him the entire story, while he stood patiently, holding Bridget in his arms. When I came to the part about Father threatening to go to the authorities, his right hand clenched into a tight fist, but still he said nothing.

However, when I was done he set his sister down, saying with great emphasis: "'Tis rubbish, Becca, rubbish the lot of it. The Connel brothers are in prison after trial, and James Ryan is already hanged for the murders at least three weeks since."

I gasped and Sean took my hand. "He went to the scaffold with these bitter words: that he wished he'd obeyed the teachings of the Church so he wouldn't be like to die. There is no better confession than that, and say your father what he will, no one will listen to him."

"You saw him hang?" I asked. Sean nodded. "Were you not afraid?"

"Fear of death takes a great deal of imagination, Becca, and I'm sorry to say I have not much of it remaining these days."

His fingers were now wound so tightly about mine they hurt. Yet I scarcely noticed the pain, so appalled was I that the youth I had seen at the wake was himself already buried. "There is so much dying in this place," I said, "that we will never be rid of it."

"Walk with me a while," said Sean, and I gladly consented, content to leave our subject matter behind, and wishful of spending more time with him without fear of the outcome. For try as he might, I believed Father was now helpless against our friendship. "I have something to tell you else, before we catch up to my sisters. The final Gale day has come and gone and I couldn't make the rent, though I've pawned every damned thing I could lay my hands upon: clothing, my pipes and, forgive me, Becca, the doll I supposed you meant for Bridget. I've tried like the devil to find work, but I couldn't even get my name on the relief rolls, smashing stones for the public works."

"Just as well. It would have killed you, as it has scores of others." Loosening myself from his tight grip and delving into my purse, I pulled out the sovereign from Christmas, still wrapped in newspaper. "I do not have the rent to give you, Sean. I have nothing near the amount you need. But I still have this, and four more shillings besides, and these you must take if you are to survive these sorrowful times." So saying, I held the coins up to him.

He stood looking at the money, undecided, but at last turned away from it. "You are so unbelievably obstinate," I went on, frustrated.

"Adamant is the better word," he replied.

"Pig-headed, rather! Why do you persist in telling me these things if you will not allow me to help?" Walking in front of him again, I attempted angrily to push the coins into his hand.

"Whom else should I confide in? And 'tis not pig-headed I am, Madam, merely determined." He was being playful now, almost laughing as he continued to deny me.

"Use your determination then, if it is so important to you, to keep yourself and your sisters alive," I cried, infuriated. "What use is it if you all die because of your idiotic stubbornness and pride? Why should a few shillings stand between us, if they keep you from your grave? You stupid dim-witted fool, cannot you understand? What matters my own life if you are dead?" Sean stopped smiling and stared at me, astonished. I perceived immediately that I had gone too far and drew back in shame, dropping my hand.

"A loan we shall call it then, Miss," said he, lifting my hand graciously and sliding the money from it. "An advance against better times." He touched his lips to my palm, afterwards turning my fingers over and kissing my ring. "I am forever in your debt, Becca. But you knew that already."

That evening, as I served dinner to Father and Sarah, spooning the vegetables and meat onto their plates and wondering again why we still had so much, I remarked casually that James Ryan and his cronies had all been apprehended and successfully tried for the murder of Mrs. Woodlock and the middleman.

"Be that as it may," replied Father, as I sat down opposite him and picked up my fork and knife, "it does not prove that others are not guilty. God only knows who else may have been involved in this conspiracy. Your ignorant peasant, for example."

Sarah laughed immoderately, but I sat quite still and swallowed a mouthful of food before answering. "My 'ignorant peasant,' as you so courteously term him, reads both Latin and Greek, taught him, I believe, by a National Schoolmaster."

"Well, well." Father looked at me thoughtfully whilst he stirred his tea. "As long as we may conclude that he does not read them to you, Daughter."

Talking to Father was akin to playing a difficult game of chess, and I considered my next move carefully. "I have never been tutored in those languages, to my recollection."

"Then we may also safely conclude that he is better educated than you are. Intellect, however, is no great gauge of innocence." Checkmate. "I have invited Mr. Cohen and the Benaris for the first *seder* of Passover, Rebecca. There will be eight to dine. Make sure that all is prepared."

15

As Sarah's wedding gown was ready, I showed it to Mrs. Benari when she came to the house to help with the demanding preparations for Passover. She admired inordinately the dove grey silk with its tiny pearl buttons and fell into raptures over the wide sleeves. "Do not you love it?" she asked Sarah. "Do not you love this pretty clothes?" But Sarah was engaged in rushing from one room to another in search of spiders, and also in discovering and touching as she went all the cracks in the walls, so Mrs. Benari turned her attentions to my future. Whilst we chopped the dried fruit for *charose*s, she leaned across to me, remarking in her heavily accented English, "It soon will be your turn to wed, Miss Rebecca, if I not mistaken. I have a younger brother, a very good man."

There seemed no appropriate answer to this. As I was not prepared to entertain what appeared to be a proposal of marriage via a third party, I retreated to the scullery to fetch a little wine to mix with the fruit. When I returned, Mrs. Benari was seated at the table with the charoses in front of her and a knowing expression on her face. "My brother, he comes soon from the continent. Already I have tell him much about you."

I struggled to maintain calm as I poured the wine into the bowl, mixing the contents with a long-handled wooden spoon. "I cannot leave my father, Mrs. Benari. He depends on me for everything domestic."

"There are ways and ways, Miss Rebecca. You cannot to stay in your papa's house forever." She sat back smugly on her seat, no doubt congratulating herself on having already organized the match to everyone's satisfaction. I understood these attempts at finding me a marriage partner were just beginning. We were such a small community that all reasonable efforts must be made to accommodate those within it and to ensure future generations. If I turned down Mrs. Benari's brother someone else's hand would be offered me, then someone else's, on and on forever until an acceptable match was arranged and Father's wrath was eased. Or perhaps he would force me.

It frightened me to imagine myself married to anyone but...I did not dare entertain the notion further, even to myself, because it seemed rebellious, perhaps even sacrilegious. However, marriage to someone unknown really did frighten me, for I imagined the state as a continuation of my present cold existence, and I dreaded it. But if it was not what I wanted, what would suffice in its place? Intimacy perhaps, warmth, love. Were such things possible?

I turned my back on Mrs. Benari and walked over to the cupboard. "I will need to extend the charoses with turnip, as we have no nuts at all, and we can use that for the *karpas* also. Do you concur?" She nodded. "We have no lamb shank for the Seder plate either, Mrs. Benari," I continued, before she could return to the question of marriage. "Should I use chicken bones instead?"

That evening there were eight of us at table, as Father had predicted. I had extended the two extra leaves, but we were still a crush. The heat was almost intolerable, as the fire and the stove were both burning, and there were simply too many bodies squeezed into too small a space for comfort. None of the guests seemed to object, however, so occupied were they in greeting and congratulating one another, and asking one another how they did.

The Seder plate took pride of place. As I glanced down at the *maror*, almost tasting in my imagination its pungent bitterness, I contemplated the wretchedness we had all witnessed and endured since our last Passover. But Mrs. Benari and I had combined our resources to produce a fine meal, and Mr. Cohen had brought an ample supply of wine. There would be no second Seder this year. We simply did not possess the wherewithal. "Next year you all to come to me," said Mrs. Benari. "Then you see what is a proper Sephardic Seder."

The service commenced, though it would have been better if we could have tied Sarah to her seat. The wine exerted a thoroughly negative influence on her behaviour. At every interval she was up and swooping around the room like a hawk, laughing intemperately, with Mr. Cohen following after her in alarm. "Won't you come and sit down, my angel," he would say. "You will merely tire yourself." But she could hardly stay seated for a moment and her erratic behaviour was making me extremely nervous. Added to my discomfort was my guilt at the magnificent meal we would serve later. My agitation only increased as the service unfolded.

"Remember now," said Father to the youngest Benari, Josef, as we advanced to the recitation of the ten plagues which were visited on Egypt, "you must spill a little of your wine onto your dish as I name each plague." And so he began to call out in

Hebrew the litany of disasters, from blood, frogs and vermin, to the slaying of the first-born. Wine dripped onto plates at appointed intervals. Sarah soared and plummeted with her betrothed lumbering in her wake. The heat in the room climbed to boiling point. Suddenly I could bear it no longer. Pushing my chair back, I rose and lifted my cup high.

"What of the plagues God has visited on Ireland?" I cried, almost hysterical. "Are we not even now in Biblical times?" And I began a catalogue of my own, dashing at each mention of a scourge my cup of wine onto the table cloth, so that bright red droplets sprayed everywhere, stains shimmering across the table like blood. "Blight...Famine...Starvation...Flood...Blizzard... Black Fever...Scurvy...Death...Death...Death."

"Death...death...death," echoed Sarah softly, retreating to her chair. Father sat staring at me with his mouth open, but Mr. Benari, who clearly thought me madder than my sister, pulled a napkin over his right hand and pushed me back into my seat, all the while trying to administer water to me with his left. I choked at his efforts and liquid cascaded down my chin.

"Have I said something wrong?" I demanded. "Is this not the truth?"

There was afterwards such a hush in the room I could hear the soup simmering on the stove. I reflected with little regret that perhaps Mrs. Benari no longer considered me excellent marriage material. "You must forgive Rebecca," apologized Father belatedly. "She has worked far too hard these last days."

"Of course, of course," replied Mr. Cohen, rushing to my side and refilling my cup. "You need to take more rest, *meine kind*."

"How thankful we must be to God, the all present, for the good He did for us," Father continued, subdued, as he resumed the service. *"Da-yaynu."*

16

The first segment of the ritual and the meal were finally over. After Father had poured the goblet of wine for *Eliahu*, he requested that I open the back door to receive the prophet. "The air will do you good, Rebecca. Stay outside for a few minutes if you have a mind."

I walked slowly into the scullery. Exhausted by the long prayers and excitement, I had barely been able to swallow a mouthful when Mrs. Benari, her daughter Judita and I had at last finished serving the food to the men and sat down ourselves to eat. I felt faint from the wine also; there had been far too much of it, and it had been too quickly consumed.

As I lifted the latch and opened the door a crack to admit the fresh air and the prophet, a hand from outside clasped mine and drew me around to the blind side of the house. "I knew sooner or later you would come out—to get rid of refuse or to visit the privy. I went to the soup kitchen today to find you, but you made no appearance."

"I go only on Mondays and not this week at all, for it's Passover. Suppose you had grasped someone else's hand by mistake?"

"I was watching through the window before you opened the door. I had to see you tonight, Becca." Sean's eyes, great and luminous in the dark, were as sad as I had ever seen them.

"What is it?" I asked, almost swooning as the cold air hit me.

He wrapped his arms around me to shield me from the chill. "'Tis terrible news I bring, my dear."

I was sober immediately, frightened at what he might have to say. "Why, what's the matter? Tell me at once."

"I do not know how to break it to you." He stood with his chin pressed against my cheek, gathering in himself the strength to continue.

"Please," I said, "you have to tell me now. Dreading what you have to say must surely be worse than hearing it."

"The landlord wishes to rid himself of my family, Becca, and so he has devised a way to evict us all whilst lessening his guilt. He has given me tickets, through his agent, which I have in my pocket now, to sail with the girls to Lower Canada. And the worst of it is, the very worst of it is, when I think on't, the blessed things cost three guineas each, with half price for the children. So he could have forgiven us what we owed on Gale day and been none the worse off."

"Why would he do such a thing? Why should he evict you?" I demanded, trying to hold back my tears.

"The bastard wants to clear the land of the potato people, as he calls us, so he'll have larger tracts to farm. That's where the money is, Becca; we're just in the way. And I would go gladly, ease myself out of the whole damned system, if it weren't that I am deathly afeard of the water, and if it weren't for..."

"What?"

"If it weren't for you." We stood looking at each other, anguished, until he leaned down, and I thought for a moment he would kiss me. I put my hand up to his lips, saying quietly, "No, Sean, it is forbidden, and I must not."

He flung himself away from me at once. "Damn it. Damn everything. By all that's holy, Becca, I don't know how to find my way out of this mess."

"When do you sail?"

"June 3rd on the bark Elizabeth," he replied with great bitterness. Father was still intoning the Hebrew prayers within, and the ghostly sound wafting through the darkness reminded me I must soon return. It was beginning to snow again, and the delicate flakes fell upon us like manna. "I cannot stand to lose your friendship. I cannot," he continued desperately.

"Nor I yours, Sean. But we must try to be sensible. There will be a new...start for you in Canada, the...chance to possess your own land and settle down..." I was trying to speak between sobs when mercifully he interrupted me.

"I will never marry," he said fiercely.

"Shall you not?"

"Never. And when people ask why I shall respond, 'Once I knew a beautiful maiden for five minutes and a hundred years, and when we parted did she not entirely seize my heart, so there was nothing remaining but a shard of ice within me?'"

He pulled me back into his arms, and as we clung together a second time I would have willingly kissed him, had Father not called out that very moment from the table, "Rebecca, come along in now and close the door behind you. Perhaps the prophet will deign to visit us another year."

"I must go. I have to, or we shall be discovered," I whispered, dragging myself away from Sean and wiping my eyes.

"When shall I see you again?"

"I cannot tell. There is the rest of Passover to consider and Sarah's wedding, but soon, soon, I promise. Soon." I ran into the house and shut the door, shaking the snow from my hair.

17

*B*ut it was not soon.

The blizzards returned, followed by torrential rains, and to my list of plagues I might have added hurricane and hail, for the winds and precipitation in April were worse than anything within living memory, and our roof was half blown away by the storms.

I was thus confined to the house for the greater part of the month, imprisoned with Sarah and Father. Sarah was impatient and fidgety, Father angry and miserable, having given up almost all hopes of selling jewellery for the time being. "There is no trade," he would complain, whilst poring over his accounts, urgently searching for another sovereign or guinea to defray the costs of the wedding.

"Why is it Mr. Cohen still wishes to marry my sister?" I asked him one day. "Her conduct at the Seder was deplorable."

"And yours was not much better, as I recall. But why should he not?" inquired Father, after he had got over his initial irritation at the question. "He blamed mild inebriation, a little too much drink, if I am not mistaken, for her restlessness. Besides, she is a beautiful, accomplished girl, and he is a generous man who loves her."

Accomplished she might be, but not at anything approaching suitable for a wife. She did not embroider, nor play an instrument, nor draw. And although these talents were not excessively important in our circle, her housewifely skills were likewise all but non-existent. Everything, however, would have been forgivable had she simply been sane, but, as things were, I could see only tragedy coming out of the marriage. It was as though we all of us sailed too close to the wind, without fear of impending disaster. Although Sarah for the most part sat quietly when Mr. Cohen honoured us with his presence, Father and I had been subjected to her screaming tantrums on more than one occasion lately.

"He does not know, he may not understand, never having seen her at her worst. I could not even cut her hair for the wedding; she pulled the shears from me today and almost succeeded in stabbing me with them."

"He rescues us from poverty. All other considerations are secondary." Father gazed into the fire as if tormented. "I do my best for each of you. I am both Mother and Father in this house."

Despite my misgivings, however, Sarah was peaceful on her wedding day. She allowed Mrs. Benari and me to dress and comb her, and looked altogether ethereal in the grey silk gown, her long fair hair partially hidden by a diaphanous veil. Father provided me with a new outfit also, a rose silk bodice with a woollen skirt in the same shade as Sarah's costume, and Mrs. Benari had managed to tame my unruly hair by sweeping it up and securing it with a pearl pin. She was kindly enacting the role of a mother, and I appreciated her presence, if not her never-ending chatter.

But if Sean could see me now, what would he think? The distance between our worlds had widened substantially this morning, as I was moulded into the pattern of a fine and wealthy lady. Though I had rather worn rags if only I could have been with him once more.

Mrs. Benari and I spoke encouragingly to Sarah whilst escorting her to the rabbi in a carriage, but she responded little at first. When we were almost halfway there, however, she turned to me quietly and requested to know where we went. "Why, to your wedding, your wedding, of course, Miss Sarah," broke in Mrs. Benari gaily, "and a wonderful day it is for the surest. You have on your prettiest clothes and they is quite lovely on you. There is not a girl in the town who can holds a candle to you this morning."

"Where is Tata?" asked my sister, as if waking from a dream.

"He has gone before us to witness the signing of the marriage agreement, Sarah. Do you not remember?" I inquired. She nodded and ventured nothing further, but I felt horribly uneasy as we arrived at our destination and helped her from the carriage.

As she stood in the small room with us where the ceremony was to take place, her hands, like mine, firmly supporting my sister, Mrs. Benari nodded to where the men were congregated, saying, "That is my brother Mr. Bernardo with the high black hat, the brown beard. He is as handsome as plainly you can to see, Miss Rebecca, and he comes here this day to look on your beauty also. I am saying for sure another wedding soon, and will speak to your father about it."

I glanced over to him; about two or three and thirty, tall and serious, Mr. Bernardo might make a wonderful husband—for somebody else. I would hardly wish to burden him with a wife whose affections were engaged elsewhere, however hopeless the attachment. He smiled faintly at me, and I looked away.

We led Sarah to the chair where the ceremony would commence. Suddenly she started as if she had seen a ghost, and began to mutter, "No, this cannot be; no, I have forgotten my *sheitl*; the veils will obstruct my view. Up or down, up or down, why can't they make up their minds? Why am I in this place anyway with all these men? We should have paid more for the wedding. My corsets are far too tight," and so on, her words becoming clearer as she walked, until the entire room was witness to her disjointed and embarrassing remarks.

"Hush now," I whispered, noting the expressions of dismay on the faces of Mr. Cohen and the assembled guests.

"Where is my groom?" she shouted. "What does he whilst I wait? Let him step forward, if he but recognizes me." We sat her down with some difficulty in the appointed chair.

Mr. Cohen, who was clothed in an ivory *kitel* according to tradition, moved towards her with apprehension, remembering himself enough at the last moment to pull her veil down over her face as the rabbi sang in Hebrew: "Our sister, be thou the mother of thousands of myriads."

"What nonsense is this? Where is my groom, I say? It cannot be that man, for he is dressed in white, and my betrothed wears a black frock coat. Can no one answer me? Where is the canopy? Why am I not under it? Tata, Tata, I thought you wished me to marry, but there is no groom here and no coin in my hand." Lifting the veil again, then biting Mrs. Benari hard on the finger and pushing my hand away with a snarl, she jumped up precipitously and threw her arms in the air as though praying to the Almighty.

"The jeweller's mad daughter...what can you expect?" I heard someone whisper, just as Sarah gave a single blood-chilling scream. "I see you now, my husband," she shrieked, pointing to the ark. She ran like lightning through the guests to a little room at the front, her long veil trailing in her wake, her wide sleeves floating out behind her like angels' wings. The door slammed, and there was silence.

"The ring is not yet on her finger," said Mr. Cohen faintly. "There is no marriage."

"That is a matter for interpretation," responded my father. "The contract is signed."

Mrs. Benari was holding her bloodied hand and crying. The rabbi had disappeared. Out of the corner of my eye I noticed Mr. Bernardo turn and walk swiftly from the room.

18

Whether Sarah was married or not was a matter for the rabbi, or perhaps even the rabbinical courts, to decide. In the meantime Father and I took her home, there being nowhere else for her to go. The wedding feast sat on the table untouched, as not a single guest would venture into our household. Perhaps it was a good thing, for how could I have run about serving them whilst trying to look after my sister? Mrs. Benari, who had been so sociable before the wedding, was invisible after it, and the three of us were thus left to shift as well as we could for one another. Our other acquaintances were clearly all fair-weather friends also, for we saw not one of them. Finally a letter arrived from the rabbi, and we knew Sarah was back in our family permanently.

In a matter of hours, my sister's extreme agitation deserted her. Perhaps aware for the first time of what she had done, she retired to her bed and stayed there, curled up in the coverlet and crying. Father, too, was sunk in melancholy and barely ate or slept. "We shall be ruined, ruined," he groaned. "All this outlay and nothing to show for it. What kind of life have I, with one daughter mad and the other rebellious? One who cannot marry, and the other who in all likelihood will not?"

"Will not? Will not? Am I not tainted by her unstable character, also? I shall never find a groom after this, Father, as you well know."

"How convenient, daughter, that you may now blame the results of your disobedient nature on your sister." He said nothing further, only glared at me from his place by the fire. Irritated by his complaints, I banged the tray down and cleared the last remnants of the wedding feast from the table with a loud clatter. We had eaten this food at every meal to save expenditure, but it had gone rotten quickly, as the weather had turned warm in early May. Scraping the ruined victuals into a pail angered me greatly, for I could not abide such waste, and it focussed my mind on Sean again. The money I had given him weeks ago for food could scarcely have lasted until now.

I had not seen him since Passover. Indeed there seemed not a trace of him anywhere: not in the yard, not in the town, not at the soup kitchen. I fretted about him constantly as I dusted and cleaned, washing the floors and spilling out the slops. Soon he would be gone for good, and I would never, ever see him again. It seemed impossible. I saw the future stretching like a huge black wall in front of me. We had not even had the opportunity to say goodbye to each other.

As the time of the sailing approached I became almost sick with worry and resolved, having had no better notion, to go up to his home when I was supposed to be assisting at Mrs. Andrews'. Feeling more than a little guilty at my scheme, I nevertheless managed to excuse my actions on the grounds that I was still helping the poor and, more important, Father would be expecting my absence on a Monday and would the more easily let me go.

I got together some small provisions and equipment Sean might need for the journey. I would almost certainly not have the chance for another visit, and I had heard the captains of the barks that plied the Atlantic were not overly generous in giving out rations to those in steerage. Collecting some oats, a little Indian corn and a few vegetables, together with a cup, a knife, and a small pot, I made ready to leave the house.

"What is this?" roared Father, peering into my basket and pulling out a turnip. "Here we have not enough money to buy food and you are dragging it away."

"It is for the soup kitchen, Father. How ever little we will have, the poor souls there have less." How skilful I had become at lying these last months! I scarcely blushed at this monstrous falsehood. Besides, I was not misled by Father's protests. His playing the outraged pauper carried little weight with me. We might have less than before with the marriage going awry, but it was still a sufficiency, and would always remain so, I believed.

"Leave the basket where it is, my girl, if you have intentions of going out. And do not 'but' me. I am determined in the matter."

Reluctantly, I did what I was bid and, wrapping my shawl around me, departed the house. I made sure to turn right out of the gate in the direction of the soup kitchen, for in all likelihood Father was watching. No sooner had I reached the corner, however, when I changed course and headed straight for Sean's. I was so impatient to see him I was willing to accept almost any risk.

I reached the crest of the hill where we had once stood together and looked down upon the city. The weather was warm and pleasant, wildflowers beginning to bloom again after the punishing winter. It was hard to imagine poverty and want on such a day. Gazing at the long sweep down to the ocean, I could see the tall sailing ships docked at the wharves, their masts like Christian crosses against the blue sky. Perhaps one of those boats was the Elizabeth, waiting to take on passengers and carry Sean across the ocean. The time was so close now. How would I manage without him? "My friend, my one true friend," I whispered, before continuing on my way.

I hoped most fervently I would find him or his sisters at home, but the shock that awaited me was overwhelming. Derelict, burned out, its outside blackened, its inside merely a mass of cinders, the cabin had clearly been deserted for several weeks. The entire place was abandoned, in fact, though I noticed with odd intensity the green shoots and leaves of a few potato plants on the hill, their delicate white blossoms swaying slightly in the breeze. They had come up without planting, flourishing from a fragment of potato left in the earth on a previous year. How strange it was they should grow now, unbidden, when the family had gone.

But what of Sean? What could have happened to him? My mind was almost paralyzed with fright at the possibilities. I walked to the corner of the house and called out his name, not expecting any answer. However, there was a slight rustle from behind the cabin, and I clearly heard the name "Becca," returned softly in response to my call. I swung around, enormously relieved and grateful, but hands grabbed my shoulders harshly from behind and dragged me away from the house.

"If it's not the mad woman's sad sister! Looking for our Sean, is it? I knew I would find you here sooner or later, if I just had the patience. Becca, Becca; I've heard him call you that so many times I could vomit." It was Spider Fingers. He was half speaking, half whispering, with a disgusting snake-like hissing, into my ear. "So how does it feel to be at the mercy of others for a change, Re-becc-ah?"

"Let go of me," I cried, "you...you creature. I know it was you who lied to my father about Sean, and I will have nothing to do with you." I shook myself free of his hold and began to scramble urgently back up the hill.

He came after me, seizing my hands and throwing me down to the ground, muttering savagely all the while: "And s'ppose it was, s'ppose it was, Re-becc-ah? He needs his comeuppance, that lad, and he has finally received it. Evicted this three weeks gone, run by the agent off the land, though he fought like the very devil. He tried to best the landlord, but now has been bested by him. Mighty flirt that he is, he can't now get near the one thing he wants most in this world. You, Re-becc-ah, you." I struggled violently to free myself, but he soon clamped me down again. "And meanwhile you don't even notice me, don't even know my name. Do you? Well, do you?" His face contorted with rage, he pulled my hair hard until I was looking right at him.

"No," I gasped, in dread and loathing. I'd always thought him pathetic, but now I knew him to be ferociously dangerous.

"It's Patrick. Say it for me. Patrick." I remained stubbornly silent, and he pulled my hair again until it felt like a million tiny nails driven into my skull. "Say it, damn you."

"Patrick," I sobbed at last.

"Now say you'll forgive me for telling your da, and I might let you up."

Alarmed that he might torture me again, I answered with immense disgust, "I...forgive you...Patrick."

"Louder," he cried, and I had to repeat the awful words to his satisfaction. Grudgingly he allowed me to stand, pulling me to my feet then stroking my cheek with his skinny fingers. I twisted my face away from him, sickened, but he said, sighing, "Your giving Sean every little bit of food or money you came by without a moment's thought for the rest of us near killed me with jealousy. Didn't you know I always wanted what he had?"

I shook my head, trying to anticipate his next move. What would he do with me now? But the attack, savage and unprovoked as it was, seemed over. Spider Fingers stood in the middle of the field, breathing heavily, the cabin hulked behind him like a ruinous black skeleton. "Go back to your house," he murmured, to my intense astonishment, "and contain your heartbreak. I'll see the miserable wretch on the boat, if he has survived these last few weeks, for the landlord has paid my passage, too. Don't worry, Re-becc-ah, I'll be sure to bid him your loving farewells, in the best way I know how."

This last was ominous, but I did not dare to reflect on it, running away from him like the wind. I felt how Isaac must have felt, knowing himself about to be sacrificed and then mysteriously released. Spider Fingers was not done with me, however, and raced after me, catching my arm. "I forgot," he grinned. "What have you in your purse?"

I dug into it, my hands trembling. "Eight pence ha'penny."

"That's all? Not much for such a wealthy young lady. Well, give it to me anyway." As he grasped the money, he let me go, and I stumbled away up the hill as fast as I could. "I will miss you, Re-becc-ah," he called after me as at the top I turned and looked back on him.

"Well, I shall not miss you, and I will never forgive you, never," I screamed, "neither for lying to my father nor for what you have done to me this day." Then I flew in terror all the way home, imagining him close behind until I slammed the door.

19

If I was afraid to emerge from my house for several days, it was scarcely surprising. As Spider Fingers had held me down in the field I had prayed that someone, anyone, might come along and save me. With his tenacious grip, starved and weakened though he appeared, he was still far stronger than I could ever hope to be. But Sean was gone, and Father had thought me at the soup kitchen. I was thus justly rewarded for the stupid falsehoods I had fallen into of late. Better perhaps to tell the truth and accept the consequences than to lie and find myself in such a perilous position in the future.

How I had emerged from my experience without permanent harm I really did not know. I could only suppose that God, who had stayed the hand of Abraham, had also been active in saving me. From this understanding, a little of my former faith slowly trickled back into my soul. I was still deathly afraid, however, and now a desperate battle raged within me—should I stay in and avoid Spider Fingers or go out and find Sean? If the latter, I would have to tell Father once and for all what I did. For the only place I might find him was on board ship, and the Elizabeth was not due to sail on a Monday. And if I did go to the ship, I went towards Spider Fingers, too.

When I returned to the house my basket still remained on the table where I had left it. I quickly gathered it up and took it to my room, hiding it sideways under the bed. Later, when I had calmed somewhat, I wondered what else Sean would need for the crossing. More food? Linens and soap? I had heard that the ships, most of which carried timber on the way back from the colonies, were filthy, and the dirt increased tenfold as the voyage went on.

I prayed in my heart Sean still lived, for I knew only too well that the poor had often disappeared into the countryside during the famine, never to re-emerge. As I compiled a list of necessities in my head over the next few days, willing him to survive, I realized my decision was made, and I would somehow go and try to meet with him and his sisters at the docks.

Accordingly, I rose on the appointed day. After serving and clearing luncheon, I took up my basket and prepared to go down to the port. I was resolved to say little to Father, although as it turned out, he had plenty to say to me.

"Where do you go?" he began, innocently enough. But my sparse response of "out," as I arranged my shawl around my shoulders, hardly pleased him. He asked the question again, louder and with obvious anger. I was still much afraid of crossing him, yet told him the truth. He countered, as I might have expected, with threats to strike me if I might only go forward to him (I would not), and a severe warning that if I persisted in my intentions he would have the constabulary arrest Sean before he could leave the city.

We had had this conversation before and his intimidation

now held little sway with me, for all the guilty parties had by this time been hanged for the crime of killing the middleman and Mrs. Woodlock. "I should have thought you would want him out of Ireland. But do what you will, as shall I," I replied softly, retreating hastily out of the back door and going on my way. He banged the door violently behind me.

There was something I needed to do before proceeding to the port, however. I wanted to retrieve Sean's Uillean pipes if I could and present them to him, for what could be more of a tragedy for him than the loss of his music? It was like a small death, and I knew I would be lost indeed if deprived of my violin.

Shmuel Cohen's was the only pawnshop on our side of the town. As Sean knew Mr. Cohen, I assumed he would have gone there after Christmas to pawn his pipes and other effects. I had little money to give the pawnbroker, however, and I was in addition most upset at the prospect of seeing him. The poor man had been so humiliated at his own wedding that he would hardly wish to encounter any member of my family ever again. In the end, though, there seemed nothing else for it, so I walked along the small enclave of shops, halting a few yards from the entrance of the pawnshop to acquire the daring necessary to enter.

It was a beautiful day, as almost every day had been this last month. I supposed the interior of the shop must have been quite stuffy, for within a moment or two of my stopping, Mr. Cohen was in the open doorway, breathing the outside air deeply and smiling at the gentle warmth of the early afternoon. I was quite abashed to see him this way. The man believed himself alone, and I felt I intruded on his privacy. But in a moment he half turned and saw me, and I was most surprised when he called out, "*Meine kind, meine kind*, how wonderful to see you. Have you come all this way to visit me?" I nodded, startled by his friendliness. "I have been meaning to come up to your house to visit your father, and see how your sister does, but I have not, excuse me, had the courage until now. It was a terrible thing, the wedding, a shocking and disappointing event, though nobody's fault when you come right down to it. Pass inside, Miss Rebecca, if you can stand the crush, but watch the dirt against your pretty skirt."

I walked in, curious to see where he spent his days. The shop was indeed crowded, filled with articles both large and small of every shape and description. Basins rested upon drawers, beds rubbed shoulders with wash stands, kettles stood on tables instead of hobs. There was clothing, too, and lanterns, and other bric-a-brac, each jostling for attention in the little room. All in all, the place looked welcoming, if somewhat disordered, and smelled of friendly dust.

"It is kind of you to receive me after what happened," said I, quite overwhelmed by the variety of goods and the cordiality of their temporary owner.

"On the contrary, it is kind of you to come. I would never have wished to lose touch with you. Now, why are you here? I can hardly hope it is merely to visit an old bachelor like myself."

I told him of my mission. Though he looked somewhat surprised, he murmured that Sean was an upstanding young man, and that I had been correct in supposing he had left the pipes with Mr. Cohen for safekeeping, as he put it. There were a number of other articles, too, he went on, bringing out some girls' dresses and a man's jacket, and my dear old peg doll, who looked a little down at the mouth at having been left alone for so long. "The period of the pawn agreement has now expired," he said, "so anybody may purchase these from me. Even you, *meine kind.*"

"I have little money to give you, sir," I began, "But I had hoped you might accept my ring in return for the pipes and the other goods. It is gold, I believe."

"Did your father not give you this ring?"

"Yes, Mr. Cohen, for my thirteenth birthday."

He looked carefully at it, squinting at the dainty ruby which was its centrepiece, and asking me if I was certain I wished to part with it. I replied in the affirmative. "It is a very good gem," he remarked. "I could give you twelve guineas for it."

"That much? Surely not?" It seemed like a fortune, altogether too much for such a small item.

"Definitely. And the things here given up by the young man will cost you two shillings if you want them, for I'm reasonably certain nobody else will. That leaves you with twelve pounds and ten shillings, which I have little doubt you will pass on to him also. Do we have a deal, *meine kind*?"

I stared at him, unable to believe his generosity. Sean had been right on that night so long ago when he called him a kind man, although I had railed at his comments at the time. Shmuel Cohen was a true and honest gentleman. I realized with a kind of astonishment that I might have done a lot worse for myself than to have been really betrothed to him. "We have a deal, Mr. Cohen, and thank you."

He brought out a small tin trunk and emptied both the contents of my basket and the articles on the counter into it, saying he would like to give it to Sean as a present, so that he could start his new life off well. Then he went to his cash drawer and withdrew the money he insisted was owing, placing it in an envelope and then into my hands. "You can call back for your basket at any time, my dear," he said genially as I put the envelope in my purse. "I promise not to sell it! Give the young man my best before he sails." Mr. Cohen looked at me as closely as he had earlier examined the ring, remarking, "You care for him very deeply, do you not?" I nodded.

"Then I'm sorry he leaves, though it is perhaps for the best in the long run. Different worlds, different worlds. But life can be very painful at times, although only God in his infinite wisdom understands the plan of things." He asked me to remember him to my father and sister, promising he would soon visit to "square up" with them, as he put it. Then he saw me out of the shop and handed me the keys to the trunk, after first enquiring whether he could bear it to the port for me. But I took it myself, though it was rather heavy and difficult to drag. Suddenly realizing from the low position of the sun that I had spent too much time with him, I made haste down to the docks, so I should not miss the Elizabeth altogether.

20

The wharf was a flurry of excitement. Passengers came and went, whilst tradespeople stood on the docks to sell provisions to them. Watched suspiciously by most were the groups of merry and raucous British soldiers, their red uniforms offensive to many of those gathered about. To the poor, these men represented, like the constabulary, the landlords and the English government, and as such they liked them not one bit. As I opened my purse to purchase more foodstuffs, herring, bacon and biscuit for Sean's trip, I noticed with great shock that Mr. Cohen had enclosed my gold ring in a bank note and tucked it into the envelope with the rest of the money. Well, I would return it to him tomorrow. I simply could not allow him to give everything away; but for the moment I replaced it on my finger. "Please wrap the bacon before you give it me," I told the vendor. "For to be sure I would not wish to touch it."

Sean and his sisters were nowhere to be found, but the Elizabeth sat with her gang plank still lowered, looking not at all like the kind of craft one would be happy to sail in for such vast distances. As I stared at the ship, I was brought to mind of a dreadful tale I had been told years before: that when the English banished the Jews, they sent them out into the Channel in leaky boats, so that they sank whilst still within sight of land. Gazing at this shabby bark, I wondered if there might not be a similar conspiracy to get rid of the poor in Ireland. Perhaps they were never intended to set foot in the Americas. However unhappy I had been before that Sean was to sail, I now felt at least twice so, though I tried to reassure myself.

He must be already embarked, I thought, approaching the Elizabeth. Pray God that he was, and I might see him. I began to haul the trunk, which seemed heavier by the minute, along the gangplank, but was soon greeted by a sailor with a big black face and a ready smile. He was the first African I had ever seen, immensely tall and strongly built. I was, to put it bluntly, extremely frightened of him, though he seemed happy enough, if not entirely helpful.

"Sorry, Miss, but you can't come on board. Captain's orders." His hand was on my shoulder. I shrank back.

"But I must. There is someone on your ship I have to see. I have this trunk for him."

"Sorry, Miss, but first, the ship is making ready to sail, and second, you have no ticket, or I'll wager you'd be holding it out to me. So you'll have to go ashore. Rules is rules." He graced me again with his cheery grin, his teeth being the only flash of white about his entire person, and I bethought me then a bribe might be in order. I took a crown out of my purse and pressed it into his big callused hand, marvelling at how his palm was quite as light as my own and feeling after this observation somewhat easier in his company.

"Sorry, Miss, but it'll cost you three guineas to walk across the gangplank."

"Three guineas?" I repeated in horror.

"The price of a ticket. Luckily for you, some of our passengers have not made an appearance."

I argued with him that I had no intention of going anywhere on his dreadful boat and would remove myself from it as soon as possible. But he only continued to smile, his head tilted sideways, as though he were listening to me with great attention. Finally, after he had remarked that it was certainly better to walk across the gangplank onto the boat in the harbour than to walk off it in high seas, I perceived the germ of a somewhat illogical threat and relented. Blessing Shmuel Cohen's generosity a hundred times over, I gave the sailor the required amount, whereupon he allowed me on board, even carrying the trunk for me. He lifted it as if it weighed no more than a cup of dripping and said he would be pleased to watch it whilst I went down to the hold to find my friend. He gave such an enormous grin at this last that I was quite taken, though I fancied he was perhaps making fun of me, and lost my fear of him entirely. "And when I come back...?"

"Yes, Miss?"

"Shall I have my funds returned?"

"Sorry, Miss. This money is for the captain. You have paid for your ticket and now you may stay or leave as you please. Make sure and go easy down that ladder," he warned me, pointing to the hatch. "It is most slippery and difficult for landlubbers." He sat down upon the trunk, looking as though not even a gale would oblige him to get up from it.

As I descended, the light faded. How dark and miserable it was below, the only illumination shining through the hatch by which I had just entered. I was sure there were many people in those cramped quarters, lying on the two-tiered wooden berths, though I sensed rather than saw them until my eyes became accustomed to the wretched gloom.

How would I ever find Sean here, amongst the hundreds who were gathered? I might as well look for a blade of grass in a whole meadow of turf. And I could not forget the sailor's remark that some of the passengers were missing. Perhaps, I considered with dread, Sean and his sisters were of that number. I ventured forward gingerly, tripping over boxes and bedrolls, catching with my foot a pail of water that had been set up in a narrow aisle and soaking myself. I stumbled around peering into every face, examining each jacket and cap, but nothing appeared familiar to me.

I fought my way back to the hatch, imagining I was watched by hundreds of pairs of eyes, distrustful and wary. I could not find Sean or his sisters, I just could not, yet I must not leave until I did. As the time for the ship to sail drew closer, my panic rose. If I got off now, I should certainly never see him again, and the thought was too awful to contemplate. I began to fancy also I would faint from the smell of so many bodies in such a confined area. It was already nauseating in the extreme, and what it would be like after many weeks at sea, I should not have wished to hazard a guess. Exhausted and thoroughly disheartened, I dragged myself to the ladder and held on to it.

"*A mhuirin*, your flaming hair here in this dark place ignites my soul with courage."

I turned quickly, thrilled by the sound of his soft voice. Insubstantial as a phantom in the unearthly light, his eyes deeply shadowed, his face tormented and drawn, Sean encircled me with his arms, saying, "The redcoats marched us down to the boat a day ago. I wanted to come to you but was prevented."

"I know."

He drew me back to the wide lower berth where his sisters lay sleeping, probably exhausted by their prolonged march. Sitting with me on a corner of the wooden slats, he began to speak. Asking not why I was there or how I did, he told me instead how his little family had subsisted these many weeks until allowed back into the city to board the boat. Sleeping in a cave with the girls, collecting seaweed and shellfish for them to eat when the salt-washed rocks had not already been picked clean by others, Sean had endeavoured to save until now a small sum that the agent had thrown at them to buy clothing. He had spent the main part of it instead on food they would need for the crossing.

There appeared a profound need in him to tell me of his experiences, which he appeared to offer by way of apology for his absence. So I did not interrupt him, even to express my pity at the horror they had all endured. Instead I waited quietly until he had finished his narrative, responding afterwards: "How dreadful your story. Thank God only that the weather was warmer this last month or you might all have perished. But you are now well set up indeed, and certainly will not lack in the future. I have come here today to bring you more provisions, and Mr. Cohen has helped me, adding a tin trunk and a small amount of money to my store."

I continued to try to encourage him as well as I could, for he looked quite terrible and his hand was deathly cold. I recounted to him also what had happened during his absence: the disastrous marriage and the failing of Father's business. I forgot the time in my nervous pleasure at seeing him again, and so almost every occurrence I described to him minutely, for I had no other confidant. I kept back only my horrible confrontation with Spider Fingers. I still feared he was on the ship and that Sean might kill him if he knew what had transpired. But I did ask him if he had caught sight of him.

"The thief from the market? Yes, he is on board, regrettably."

"Watch him well, then, for I mistrust him greatly," I said, moving onto other matters, such as the return of Sean's pipes, which had him almost in tears, and the necessity for him to write to me from Lower Canada, so that I should know he was well.

"But, oh, Sean," I concluded sorrowfully," I have stayed too long here, though, truly, I cannot imagine the pattern of my life without you." As I tried to stand there came from above a loud crash as though iron chains were being thrown onto the deck. A jarring tremor followed, then the boat began to rock precariously, pitching me into him. "I must go," I cried out in distress, "or I shall be caught here. Come up with me; your belongings are on deck." This was not at all the parting I had envisioned, and I could see that he too was alarmingly apprehensive, though for a quite different reason. Seizing hold of me again, he clung tenaciously to my arm. "I need you by my side, Becca. 'Tis bereft I am without you."

"I have to go, I have to. Please do not prevent me," I beseeched him, disengaging his fingers and thrusting myself forward to the ladder, quickly grasping its oily rungs so that I could pull myself up. He followed me, but as soon as I reached the deck I gasped. To my immense dismay I realized we had already travelled several dozens of yards from the shore, and the sea now lay, a deep blue obstacle, between me and the city. Several passengers were waving farewell to their relatives, and children chased one other around in glee at our departure. The African sailor was still standing near the trunk, although he was bent over the side of the ship as if better to behold the foam of our wake, and I shouted to him, "Turn the boat around, so please you, sir, for I must return to my home."

He only smiled his broad engaging smile, however, as if my request was preposterous, reminding me I had been sold a ticket and advised at the time it was my choice whether I went or stayed. I was intent on quarrelling with him, but at that moment there came a great commotion. As we looked towards the shore a number of constables raced to the part of the wharf where the ship had previously been docked. "Captain of the Elizabeth, come back," cried one of them, "for we believe you have a murderer in your midst."

"And if there is but one," called back the amiable captain, who stood a little way off from us, "I'll be much surprised." He laughed uproariously, the African sailor joined in, and as the boat shifted to accommodate a wave, I caught sight of Father, his face set in fury, his arms hanging limp at his sides with impotence and disappointment. And unless I wished to swim back to the shore, I was marooned on this ship in the gown and shawl I stood up in.

21

For a time we stayed close to land as our bark hugged the green and rugged coast of Ireland. Then we were out to open sea, and with our isolation came the awful realization that I could never return to my home, even if by some miracle it ever did prove possible. Whether Father had seen me aboard the Elizabeth I could not say, though I hoped he might have, so that at least he would not anguish over my disappearance. But my life as part of his family was over forever. I could not doubt it, for my presence on a boat for weeks with no chaperone, even if it had occurred by accident, could only be viewed as immorality of the worst kind.

Sean was very much worried for my welfare in this regard and asked me to wear my ring on my wedding finger, so that I should not be tormented by unmarried men. "And I shall not bother you, either, though they think you belong to me," he insisted. "You must share our berth, for there is nowhere else for you to sleep, and indeed I need to see you in order to protect you. But we will put all three girls between us, and I swear no harm will come to you."

After my initial shock at being trapped on the ship, and despite the fact I had now become one of the many whom I had pitied before, I must admit to feeling from time to time a small sad joy at being in Sean's company. Was that not what I had always wished for?

"In your heart, Becca, did you mean to come with me ?" he asked one day, seeking some proof of my feelings for him.

"I cannot tell. I did not think so at the time, but have ever wanted to be with you, as you well know, only wishing it could have been in better circumstances." I believe this satisfied him, and I was thus excused from explaining the myriad confusions in my mind that this strange journey had not in the least alleviated. What of my own family? My religion? My faith in God, which swung like a pendulum between conviction and disbelief from hour to hour? Fate had thrust me here for reasons of her own, and I wished sincerely that eventually she might answer some of my questions, but as it was I felt more perplexed and doubtful about life than ever before.

We had some good times at first. The girls had more food and clothing than of late and, in the evenings, Sean would take out his pipes and play slowly and softly to us. Others had brought instruments, too, and often they would join in, their sound rising from all quarters of the hold, their rhythm matching the gentle rocking of the boat. It was a nostalgia for Ireland that I heard in this music, a yearning for life as it had been before the Famine. I listened with a kind of wonder to its grace and beauty, all the while missing my violin and wishing I might join in.

Nevertheless, in spite of these magical interludes, how altogether terrible was life below deck. In my home I had been used to privacy, but here every act I performed was entirely public, with a hundred or more people looking on. Though they seemed not one whit nonplussed by the situation, I could not bear it. The smell by degrees I got used to, and the rats, though at the beginning their bristling snouts filled me with terror. So bold were the creatures that they would come right out in the open to steal from us. The filth, however, was dreadful, and as time went on it grew worse, until the floor of the hold was covered in an unwholesome muck.

Determined by habit that our little family at least would stay clean, I scrubbed our berth and the ground under it with kosher soap weekly, thanking Heaven that I had had the foresight to bring it, and with Mary's help laundered our clothing up on the deck whenever possible. The dresses returned by Mr. Cohen were a godsend, for they had been the children's Sunday garb. They still fit, though they were a little short. The girls exchanged these for the rags they had worn onto the boat, which although tattered, were now clean also. They could make do with them whilst I rinsed out their good clothes. I washed Sean's shirt as often as I could, too. But it was with my own outfit that I had the most difficulty, for if I wanted it scrubbed I had nothing else to wear. I was therefore obliged to wash it by degrees, first the skirt whilst I kept on my petticoats, and then my petticoats whilst I retained my skirt. The bodice was a little more difficult, for I wore nothing except a shift and stays beneath; still, I managed it by wrapping my shawl around my person for modesty's sake and was quite pleased with the results. We cleansed ourselves often, too, although it was with a bucket of seawater kindly handed me by Barnabas the African, because fresh water was in short supply. Consequently, our skin and clothing were sticky with salt, and the five of us reeked of the ocean. But better by far to smell of brine than dirt. I had long held that filth led to sickness, and there were many already ill in those cramped quarters.

Our rations were given to us by the captain—oatmeal and biscuit on alternating days. We took our turn cooking the oatmeal at a fireplace on deck, but there was precious little of it and less for the children, so I was heartily glad I had brought extra provisions. We ate the vegetables raw and I'm certain they did us a power of good, although when it came to the bacon I turned violently sick at the sight of it.

"Do not make me eat it," I begged Sean, but he replied only that remaining alive was more important than dietary considerations. So I did my best with it, for his sake, yet brought it back up with disgust not five minutes after choking it down. "There goes a waste," I sighed ruefully, "and someone else could have profited by it." He did not press pig meat on me again, but tried to push every other morsel of food meant for him into either my mouth or his sisters', as if we were baby birds. He would gladly have starved had we let him.

We spoke often to each other as we lay awake at night. It was not as dark as might be expected, for some of the families stuck lit candles onto the sides of their berths. We were afeard at times they would catch the whole boat on fire, but were grateful for the light. If we inched up a little above the girls and Bridget's peg doll, which she clung to with incredible persistence, I could see Sean's face quite clearly. It was a blessing to me. Despite the hundreds milling round and over us, it seemed we were alone in the world, the last people truly alive. At first, as the voyage began, we teased each other. "You were the most outrageous flirt in the world when we first met," I told him, wiser now.

"Wasn't I though?" he replied with great pride, and we laughed quietly to ourselves.

But as time went on we found we had very little to rejoice in. Encountering a harsh and freezing storm, we were shut away in the hold. The five of us wedged ourselves into a corner in the blackness so that we wouldn't be pitched into the berths as buckets and other loose articles came flying at us. The hatches were closed tight, I imagine so that the ocean should not engulf us, but still it poured in, soaking us and lapping against our feet. The ship heaved up and down, one end slicing hard out of the water and then the other. I was much frightened we would not survive and prayed to a God I was not sure was there.

This gale did not abate for many hours; but at last somewhat calmer weather prevailed, though all we could see when finally allowed on deck was a grey churning sea, the waves in slow violent motion. There was not a tree or a blade of grass, not a whisper of land anywhere, to raise our confidence. I did not know but I should have preferred for God to drown us all and put an end to our misery.

Tempers flared disgracefully after the storm. People quarrelled with one another in high accusing voices, shouting that one aboard was stealing from them, for they had lost a shilling, an oatmeal cake, or an ounce of tobacco. Although the thief might have been the ferocious weather, which flung everything everywhere, rather than any human agent, their losses were still a pity indeed, for everyone had little enough to start with.

As further time passed, the provisions became tainted, the sick aboard grew sicker, and the doctor, afraid for his own life, would not come down to them. The drift of our conversation then shifted, changed, as well it might. Our spirits plunged quickly with all these calamities.

"'Tis a tomb we travel in," Sean lamented one evening, having lost all hope. "Our final resting place." The heat was terrible below, but through the reopened hatch there shimmered a fraction of the moon, radiant and golden, and I realized that it shone not only on us but on Lower Canada, too. There would finally be an end to the voyage.

"No, Sean," I replied, although I was almost as frightened as he to be at sea for such a long and miserable trip. "We sail on Noah's Ark, and should we continue for forty days and nights, we shall still emerge on dry land afterwards." There came a glimmer of a smile to his shadowed face, and I thought drowsily, as I fell asleep, that I was perhaps Noah's wife, and we should never be parted.

On Sundays, weather permitting, the passengers climbed on deck to participate in a service. There were two, a Catholic and a Protestant. As I did not belong in either group, though Sean was particular in taking the girls each week, I would stand some way away, feeling profoundly estranged. One Sunday I caught sight of Barnabas sitting further along, his legs stuck out before him, as was the sailors' fashion. He was sing-songing to himself comfortably and mending sail with an enormous needle and thread. I walked over to him, endeavouring to keep my skirt from flying up in the brisk wind.

"Why, Miss, are you not at service?" he asked calmly, stopping his sewing to smile up at me.

"I do not belong to these people, Barnabas," I replied, feeling very sorry for myself, "yet am in a way alone here, having neither family nor religion to comfort me."

"Why, Miss, and it is the self same thing with me, having been separated from my home for these past twenty years and hardly ever catching sight of another African, or a free one, at least." He began to mend again. "But do you not have Master Sean and his sisters to be your family?"

"Yes, and they are wonderful. But they are much different from me. And there is a loneliness to that."

"It has come to me over time, Miss, that there is always comfort among people who is honest, and company also, so I'm not as lonely as I might be."

"This ship then, is your home?"

"This ship or any other. But the sailors is my friends, and the captains, and some of the passengers like yourself, wherever I be. And so I am content." He certainly looked so, for the broad grin almost never left his face, whatever unpleasant task he was obliged to engage in.

"Thank you, Barnabas. You have given me something to think on." I looked out on the ocean and was amazed to recognize at some distance another boat that plotted the same course as ours. Like a giant seabird, it rode high on the water, gliding in our wake. I watched it fascinated for some time, the splay of its sails like powerful wings in the wind, and I wondered how its passengers did. Afterwards, I returned to steerage to lie on my berth and await the end of the service.

There were a number of the sick or exhausted down there, and a baby or two, crying or sleeping, but otherwise I was quite alone. I shut my eyes, reflecting upon the city we had left, as well as upon Mr. Cohen, my father and my sister. I had begun to drift off, my thoughts a lazy spiral of dreaminess, when I heard beside me a scrabbling as of the detested rats. After a moment, a slimy voice spoke in my ear. The long drawn-out repetition of my name told me immediately who it was, and I shuddered awake. Although I had caught sight of him several times on the boat, he had until now happily left me alone.

"Get away from me or I shall scream, and Sean will come down and kill you, at the very least."

"Do not fear me, Re-becc-ah, for I do not wish you any harm, but come rather to do you some good."

"Get away, I say." I hit him hard and he retreated for a moment, returning to catch my arms in one hand and cover my mouth with the other, his disgusting fingers cutting into my flesh.

"Your lad, Sean, has planned it all, as I have heard. Prevented you from leaving so he can ransom you back to your da when we reach Canada. He'll make himself a tidy profit, if I'm not mistaken. You could be with me instead of him, Re-becc-ah, for I shall be a rich man, and you'll want for nothing. I make you this offer now." But as he paused for a moment to consider his future wealthy existence and my participation therein, I struggled against him bitterly. Remembering my sister's strategy at the wedding, I bit his hand with as much strength as I could muster. He let go abruptly, and began to curse me, but I jumped off the berth and screamed at him, and, to my immense relief, he turned and began to slink away.

"I might have been influenced by your lies once, but not now. I know Sean far too well to be affected by your vicious falsehoods, and I swear I'll kill you myself if you ever speak to me or touch me again," I cried at his retreating back. Clearly an episode such as this was the last thing he wanted, with passengers beginning to return from prayers. He vanished among them soundlessly. I sat back down, trembling with belated fear.

It wasn't until a few minutes later that I noticed the lock on the trunk was broken. Searching inside it frantically, I soon realized the rest of our money, some seven and a half pounds I had placed there for safe-keeping, was missing, as well as a part of our remaining food. I nearly shrieked with rage. But I had no opportunity to tell Sean of our loss, for at that moment he slid down the greasy ladder as if the constabulary were after him, Bridget half hidden inside his jacket. He lay her down in the middle of the berth and wrapped her in our only coverlet. Sweat glistened on her little brow; extremely pale, she was breathing in quick short bursts.

"She's so sick, Becca, too sick even to cry. I put my hand to her head at the end of the service and it felt like hot coals. Pray

God 'tis not the fever." He crossed himself, and leaned over her, desolate. By fever he meant Black Fever, which had been still raging in the city when we left. In all likelihood it had embarked with us in port, travelling beside us like an unwelcome guest despite all our measures to avoid it, and deciding at last to reveal itself. It almost always proved fatal.

22

The voyage did not take forty days and forty nights but considerably longer, though Barnabas was quick to tell me it was shorter than many he had experienced. Bridget caught the sickness on the forty-third day of our voyage, and on the fifth day afterwards, as we neared the coastline of the Americas, she broke out in a horrible blackish rash. We then knew for a certainty what ailed her.

Sean and I put the two others down at the bottom of the berth and slept on either side of her, our hands clasped over her tiny form. Other passengers pointed out our folly, saying that we would almost certainly be infected ourselves. But what could we do? She could not be abandoned, but must be loved and cleaned and given water so that she might rally, and there was no one else to accomplish these tasks.

We still spoke to each other through the endless nights, pitch black now as all the candles were used up, trying to cheer each other through our anguish. It was not long before Sean noticed some items were missing. I carefully mentioned my suspicion that Spider Fingers had stolen them, whilst recounting his malicious treatment of me. I was terrified that he might assault me again. But though Sean said he would "get him at the last," he seemed far too intent on looking after Bridget and the rest of us to pursue the matter further. Although much surprised, I was glad of it, for I did not believe him in any way robust enough to withstand a fight; he seemed now as weak as Samson with his hair cut off.

I thought the incident forgotten and put it from my mind, but a day or so later Spider Fingers passed our corner on his way up to deck. He glared at me with such a sullen expression as he went by that I shivered, and Sean was off the berth and after him in a flash. "Don't," I shouted, but he had already swung up the ladder and disappeared, despite his lack of strength. When I tried to follow, Bridget held on to me like a baby monkey, wailing that I should stay. So I sat in the eerie light with her, half-mad with worry and agitated by every sound, every sharp noise that went on above me, until Sean slipped back down. His right eye was half closed and his nose bloodied. I hurried to tear a strip off my petticoat and staunch his bleeding, rebuking him all the while for his stupidity.

"Do not scold me, for 'twas something I had to do. He will not trouble you again, Becca, of that you can be certain, but I'll be surprised if we ever see any of the money again."

"Why, what has happened to him?" I cried.

"Be still, and give yourself no further distress over the villain. He's sprawled out on the deck with a bruised head and wounded pride, after denying his savage treatment of you and all knowledge of the theft. He'll live, unfortunately, though he wouldn't if I had my way." And truly, Spider Fingers stumbled down a little later, limping with pain, averting his face from us, and we did not set eyes on him again for the rest of the voyage.

On the fiftieth day out of Ireland land was sighted. Leaving Bridget for a scant while, we struggled up to the deck, barely able to move for exhaustion. And we weren't the only ones suffering. The weariness of both passengers and crew was terrible to behold. The fever stalked us all like a hungry lion, and we could not even take comfort as we spied the rocky shore with its wind-lashed trees and bushes. The land was like a mirage. Fearing we should never set foot on it, we went below to lie once more with Bridget, willing her to remain alive until we reached our destination.

At last we reached the quarantine station of Grace Island—or Grosse Île as the French called it. We were to sojourn there for a time to avoid spreading sickness to the mainland. Having quite given up all desire to go aloft, I understood what Sean had meant when he had said one needed an imagination to fear death. As we docked, Barnabas came down to the hold.

"I am sorry, Miss and Master, but I must deliver the little one from you now," he said sadly as he tried to take Bridget from us. "She will be cared for in the sick sheds on this side of the island, whilst you will be quartered on the other, so that you may stay clear of contagion." Taking her up carefully in his big hands, as if she were made of porcelain, he picked up the peg doll, too. Ill as she was, it still brought her comfort. I was doubly affected by the sight of the huge man cradling the little child, for he was so diligent and tender in his concern for her welfare. In the main the sailors refused even to touch the sick or dead, with good reason. But Sean cried out and would not let her go, afraid he might never see her again.

"Hush, Sean. We will get settled ourselves and visit her," I reasoned with him, without much hope that this might be a possibility. "In the meantime she will be well cared for, because the captain says there are priests and doctors on shore."

He was too weak to resist for long, and Bridget was borne away from us. Others were carried out too in the sweltering heat, for a priest and several soldiers, brave souls that they were, had come down to steerage to remove them. I saw with a little pity I could not stifle that Spider Fingers was amongst the ailing. We had lain so long beside sickness: perhaps Sean had knocked the fever into him with his fist.

It was to be a full day before I saw Bridget again. Those of us who had been found free of illness were sheltered in tents near the promontory and given meat and fresh bread, the first I had eaten in almost two months. The water too was fresh, and I felt better immediately, although I was still much alarmed for Sean and his sisters. They were so much weaker than I, having been in an almost starving condition before we departed Ireland. The ravages of the trip were much evident in their faces and demeanour. In the evening the girls retired to the tent I was to share with them, and Sean and I sat watching as bonfires were lit, their smoky plumes rising like a pillar of fire high into the heavens. The brilliant stars in their differing constellations beamed their fragile light upon us.

"I will go to the sick sheds and see Bridget tomorrow," I told him, "whilst you must stay here and regain your strength."

"I cannot allow you to visit amongst the sick and dying, Becca. Your life is too valuable to me."

"As is Bridget's to both of us," I replied. He protested further, avowing he would go himself. Although I knew him too feeble to cross the island, small though it might be, I chose not to argue with him. Saying my good nights a little while later I returned to my tent, sorry to part with him, for he must sleep somewhere else. The next morning I rose as the first ribbons of dawn strung their bright colours across the sky. Taking care not to rouse either Mary or Peggy, I began the walk back along the path to the sick shed.

It would be a beautiful island when free of disease. The trees were various and stately, tall oaks and evergreens, birch and maple. They towered above me like a wedding canopy, whilst the wild flowers congregated in their fiery oranges and yellows wherever they had not been trodden down. Along the shore lichens and delicate ferns bloomed resolute amongst the rocks, their sturdy presence encouraging me to believe that we also might survive these lamentable times. We had come so far, outlived a famine and crossed an ocean in deplorable conditions. Now we too clung to these rocks, strangers in a strange land, ready to begin again.

In truth I still felt the movement of the boat. In addition my legs were weak and the walk a struggle for me. When I reached my destination they almost gave way altogether. The sight that greeted my eyes, particularly after the loveliness of the island, was frightening in the extreme. Looking back on it now, I have little wish to describe it, except to say the sick shed was full to overflowing, and the patients were spilled over into tents or even onto the bare ground. Their condition was affecting, their cries for help shocking. The plight of many of them was, I believed, beyond human intervention. But I could not even get close enough to them to search for Bridget, because a soldier approached me immediately, preventing me from going any further.

I tried to describe the small child to him, but although he seemed sympathetic enough, he could be of little help. "There are that many children here, Miss, I cannot tell one from another, except to tell you that they are all very ill."

"Then I beg you allow me through, so that I may look for myself."

"You cannot do that in any circumstances. These are not my rules but the rules of quarantine to ensure that you do not carry the sickness back to the healthy side of the island."

I turned away and walked slowly from him, but as I did so something lying in the grass caught my eye. I discerned it immediately to be my old peg doll. Running with a strength I could hardly muster to pick it up, I returned to the soldier, saying, "Here, this belongs to her. She must be somewhere close by." But he refused to be further drawn into discussion, expressing only what he knew to be the truth, namely that the child would be returned to our family if and when she recovered.

I thanked him and began disconsolately to make the long walk back across the island. As I reached a stand of trees, however, I saw what appeared to be a covering of white upon the ground, like a residue of snow that had escaped the summer's heat. Approaching closer, I realized at once that I looked upon the form of a small child and knew in my sorrowing heart that it was Bridget. She lay like an angel with the breath gone out of her—as light as an autumn leaf, as insubstantial as the seed of a dandelion clock. I was almost afraid she might be borne away on the wind at any moment. Grieving greatly, I set the peg doll next to her and went to find a priest.

"She must have been looking for us," I told Sean many days later, when the shock of seeing her little coffin lowered into a trench had worn off enough that I might talk about it. "I hold myself to blame, for although you tried to stop Barnabas from taking her, I stayed your hand."

"Oh, Becca, Becca, 'tis neither of us guilty of her death, for we both did all we could to save her." We were sitting quietly on the promontory, reflecting on the little child who had left us and regarding the steamers carry those who had survived the quarantine period up river to Quebec and Montreal. "We shall soon be leaving this place," he went on as we watched. "Thank God the rest of us continue well."

"It is a miracle, indeed." I felt I knew what he would say now, for we were to be separated—he and the girls going to Quebec City to the Catholic Orphanage, from which place they would all no doubt be placed in different homes, and I being taken to Montreal. Father Allard thought, despite the irregularity, he might be able to find me a Jewish family to stay with.

"*A chuisle mo chroi*, pulse of my heart, if 'twas love only between us I could bear it, but 'tis so much more, and we have come through so much together. *A mhuirin*, you are the twin half of my soul, and I would do anything to keep you with me."

He would never again ask me to marry him, his pride too bruised since that day in his wretched home when he had asked if I might turn Catholic; and now that we knew each other so much better he understood the agony involved in such a choice. I had thought of this moment often and with anguish over the past few days, wondering whether I would have the courage when we were close to parting to say and accomplish what was necessary for our happiness.

"Sean," I began slowly, "I have spoken to Father Allard..."

He looked up at me with extreme diffidence, though a faint ray of hope gleamed through the smoky darkness of his eyes.

"And he is willing to baptize me, so that we may wed. Then we may keep the girls with us also."

"Are you sure? Are you quite sure?" he asked, so nervous and delighted that he hardly knew how to compose himself.

"From the moment I first saw you at the market I have cared for you. My affection has only increased with time, though I have struggled against the emotion, feeling it to be wrong. But it is not wrong, Sean; I see that now. It cannot be wrong to love someone who has put my welfare always before his own, and who has endeavoured to protect me against every evil." I would say no more then, for the loss of my Judaism was a hard sacrifice for me, but I believed a worthy one. I had come at last to believe that religion was less important than faith in God and a hope that people might love one another, live peacefully, and survive to see better times. Bridget's death had taught me something of this. I knew at once by looking at Sean's dear face that I would never regret my decision. Yet if I had any abiding doubts, his affectionate embrace removed them from me forthwith.

Later, after telling the girls of our plans and having them almost dance about us with happiness, we stood together talking in an altogether more light-hearted vein. "I promise you," he said seriously, "that though you convert and be the best, the most devout Catholic in this world, never shall I keep pigs nor require you to eat pork again. But I have no ring to give you," he continued regretfully.

"It is no matter; we shall use mine. It has travelled a long way with us," I replied. And thus our betrothal agreement was sealed.

23

My Dear Father,

I cannot tell if this letter will ever reach you. I will take it down to the sailor on a timber ship when I have completed it, and as I understand him to be a good man, I believe he will deliver it to you should he have the chance when he returns to Ireland. But as to when that will be, or whether it will ever happen at all, I have no notion. I trust to God, however, that you will receive it, so that you will at least know what has occurred in my life these past months.

As to whether you saw me on the Elizabeth that day you came down to the port in June, I do not know, but in any case I was on board, having been caught by surprise when the ship sailed. I do not wish to sadden you with the details of the voyage, save to say they were worse than wretched, but once disembarked in Lower Canada I took the decision to marry Sean and live with him and his two remaining sisters, the third, Bridget, having died most pitiably after we docked.

Someone who had stolen from us also died, a boy named Patrick from the market. I believe he came to you at some point with untrue accusations about Sean. The authorities found more than a hundred pounds on his person, so we got our funds back in the end, as did others. Though I would rather he would have stayed alive and kept the money than carry his jealousy of Sean with him to the grave. There has been too much death here.

I know all these tidings will distress you deeply, particularly those regarding my marriage, but I care for Sean so much and could see no way of going on without him. In the end, I came to this conclusion: if the Marranos converted to avoid death, as you told me, why should I not convert to celebrate life? Is this not equally worthy? I am a Jew by practise; the ritual is entrenched in my bones and will live with me forever. But many months ago Sean said he believed we shared the same faith under the differing mantles of our religions. How clever he was to understand that, although I did not know what he meant at the time, not truly, not in my heart. I do now: faith is the glue that binds people together; and in my faith I am no different from any of the souls on this quarantine island, having endured so much with them. Survival has become my religion.

I hope you understand even the smallest part of what I write. I miss you, I miss Sarah, and I must tell you also that I miss Mr. Cohen, who was so kind to me the last day I was in Ireland. I hope you may have made amends to each other, and that you will give him my regards.

Sean and I will be moving with his sisters to a small community close to Quebec. We are all immigrants here and must begin a new life together.

I remain, Father, your affectionate, if not always obedient, daughter,

Rebecca

24

It was almost Christmas, more than a year later. A courting candle sat in one window, together with an ailing shamrock plant, to welcome Joseph and Mary; and a few small tapers in homemade clay holders were propped in the other, as a remembrance of Chanukah. If Sean knew that I still in some sense waited for my Messiah, whilst he had found his, he never mentioned it. And I am certain we were the only Catholic family in the area to light special candles on Friday evenings and to celebrate the Last Supper of our Lord with a ceremony akin to a Passover Seder. I tried hard to do what was expected of me, but like the Marranos of old, my Judaism was still a powerful flame that burned hot and true in my heart.

Life in Lower Canada could not be called easy by any means. There was drudgery and hardship almost always, and many complained unremittingly. But it was still a far cry from the misery and famine we, and more particularly Sean and his sisters, had left behind. If we worked hard there was enough to eat and clothing to wear. Our neighbours were helpful in teaching us the ways of our new country, even if we were slow to learn at times.

As I removed a pot of stew from the crane over the fire, my cheeks burning from the heat, I regarded my little family with affection and pride. Sean sat by the fireside in his working clothes and boots, Mary and Peggy giggled whilst they taught each other with little dexterity to twist wool into yarn on a spinning wheel, and our new baby, Sean's and mine, lay fidgeting after her feed. Sean rocked her cradle gently with his foot as I readied the meal. I believe the cunning mite would have wished for him to do this all night and half the day also, for she stopped fretting after a moment and began to coo, which I am sure she knew utterly dissolved his heart. He took her out and held her on his lap.

"She'll never sleep if you do that," I chided with mock severity. "And she'll grow up spoiled."

"Sure and that's all right then. Didn't I want her to take after her mother?" He was incorrigible, sitting there with the baby and laughing at me. He so much resembled the carefree boy I had known before our terrible adversities, that I loved him more than ever, if such a thing were possible.

"Put her back. And bring your chair to the table. We're going to eat. And don't you dare say," I warned him, imitating his accent, "that sure and you thought I'd never be done with cooking, or I shall cheerfully strangle you."

"That's the way, Rebecca," remarked Mary, setting down the wool. "Put him in his place."

"A houseful of women," sighed Sean, rolling his eyes in feigned despair. "And to think I could be a bachelor still."

"Then there'd be no one to cook and clean for you. As it is you have the three of us, and baby in training," retorted Peggy, as she sat down.

Sean took a piece of bread and chewed on it thoughtfully. "And if there were not the four of you great greedy girls to support, would I not be a happier man?"

"No," we cried in unison, all except the baby that is, who, still ensconced in her father's arms, stared from one to the other of us with a kind of unfocussed wonder. Suddenly she began to chuckle, the deep belly chortling of the very young, and her little bonnet fell halfway across her face. She looked so funny sitting upright on her father's knee with one eye hidden from us like a pirate's, that we could not withhold our mirth, and laughed till the tears ran down our cheeks. Soon Sean righted her cap along with her dignity and replaced her in her crib, whereupon she yelled for a moment with lusty indignation before giving a great sigh and sticking her tiny fingers into her mouth.

How happy we were that night, for it was Christmas Eve, with a good supper in front of us and oranges on the table. Last Christmas had been frightening indeed, with Sean and me just married and no home to speak of for the four of us. This Christmas, the last week of 1848, was a very different matter, a true celebration, despite the bitter winter and our evident poverty.

A rap sounded, so hard and sharp that it almost knocked the door off its hinges. The knock came again, even louder this time, and I stood up hastily, wiping my hands on my apron. Who could be visiting at so late an hour, with supper to be eaten and families readying themselves for Mass? "Must be the Blessed Virgin Mary and her sainted husband, looking for somewhere to lodge. And us with a baby already. Didn't I tell you not to stick that candle in the window whilst the stable is in such bad repair?" Sean grinned engagingly at Peggy, who frowned back at him as though she had no time for his brotherly teasing.

But Sean was wrong for once. It wasn't the Holy Family at all that I opened the door to but a powerful shadowy figure. As I strained in the dark to see who it was, I recognized with great shock my father, waiting with an air of extreme impatience as wet snow fell upon his hat and coat. He looked so strange, so out of place, that I could not believe at first that he was really here in Lower Canada in front of me, instead of back in Ireland where I understood him to be. I steadied myself against the doorjamb, staring at him, speechless. He was carrying my violin, which he thrust towards me, saying loudly, "I thought you might want this, so I brought it along. Aren't you going to ask me in, daughter?" But I just touched my hand out to the violin tentatively, for it was a rare treasure to me, then dropped my arm and stood there like a statue, paralysed, until Sean came to my rescue.

"Where are your manners, Becca? Will you not step inside, sir?" he asked courteously, taking the violin from my father and setting it down on the table. It was only after Father entered that I saw Sarah, who had been previously hidden behind him. As she tripped in, agitated and rapid in her movements, I could see immediately how things were with her. "Hello, Sarah," I greeted her, finally finding my tongue and determined at all costs to keep her away from the baby.

"Becky, how wonderful to see you again, though in all conscience, this was not the kind of marriage I thought you would make. Oh, you have a baby, too, I see. I do love little children. Does it crawl yet? Why if this is not the coldest country in the world, I'd like to see colder. No, that's a falsehood; in truth I would hate it. I cannot know how you manage, though I notice you have a good fire there. Is dinner finished? Might there be any food remaining to eat?" She did not await my response but, skipping over to the table and leaning over the cooking pot, pulled off her gloves and scooped stew into her mouth with her fingers.

"The food is not kosher, Sarah," Father and I called out together, but she was already back at the doorway, complaining that she needed the privy for it had been a long journey this day, and why she was here altogether she just couldn't fathom.

"I'll show her where the backhouse is," offered Peggy, her eyes round as apples. She jumped from her seat speedily and slipped out of the door with my sister. The little girl was back in a minute, rubbing her hands from the cold. Then she and Mary gawked at the other newcomer, who stood straight as a ramrod in the centre of our cabin. The baby began to fuss, Sean picked her up and cuddled her, and I at last regained my wits enough to introduce everybody.

"This is Sean, Father, as you know," I said, the muscles around my mouth so tight that I could barely form the words. I did not smile, could not have looked welcoming had my future depended on it. I still did not understand the reason he was there in our home in St. Catherine de Fossambault. The two men viewed each other warily, as if they belonged to opposing armies, and for the very first time I glimpsed Sean through my father's eyes, rough, ill-clothed, one of the enemy. But the vision vanished almost instantly and he became my own dear husband again, the person I cared for more than any other in this world, with the possible exception of our baby. "And these are Peggy and Mary, Sean's sisters and mine."

"How d'you do, sir," chorused the girls, curtsying as if it were royalty visiting.

I took the baby from Sean then and held her out to Father. "This is your grandchild, Father, a little girl. Will you not take her?"

Father sat down at the table. He took the child awkwardly into his arms, much to my surprise, and brusquely asked her name.

"It is Yochevet, after my mother. And her middle name is Bridget, which is what we call her by, from day to day." He looked deeply affected and this touched me, too, but it had been much easier to forgive him in a letter than in person. I could not work out how I felt about him after so much time. Here was the man who had looked after me as a child and had done his best by me, according to his beliefs. But his presence unleashed a great anger in me also, an emotion I had long buried and thought forgotten, for I had also been threatened and beaten by him. I could not forget either that he had sent the constabulary down to the docks to arrest Sean. How might I ever forgive such treachery, and how could he sit in this room without apology? "Why have you come, Father?" I asked. He was certainly too late if he wished to break up our marriage. But if he had visited for that purpose, I suddenly realized, why had he brought me what he knew to be the most powerful peace offering of all, my violin?

"I received your letter, daughter. I wished to answer it personally and meet your family. Besides, as you know, I am the proverbial wandering Jew, travelling from Poland to England and then to Ireland. Why not wander a little farther whilst I have the strength?" He was looking down at the baby and smiling at her, though with some uneasiness. He had never been good with children.

The mildness of his response startled me, and I realized at once he was trying to excuse himself in his own unbending way. Although I was still overwhelmingly bitter, recognizing it was not a gracious apology by any means, it was a definite endeavour to mend things, of that there could be little doubt. And then again, however angry and disappointed I might be, I could not help but soften towards him. It was a hard, hard thing for him to change, almost as difficult as it had been for me to convert. I had to respect him for doing so, no matter what his reasons. Especially, I had to admire his courage in coming all the way to us without knowing the kind of reception he might receive. He must have searched for us a long time, as the last boats arrived in October, before the river froze. Yet he did not complain of it. His habitual gruffness was now a kind of shield, a cover for his uncertainty.

It was at this juncture that he tried to make amends to Sean, turning to him and saying bluntly, with a poor attempt at humour, "Those three eggs you brought my daughter from the market cost you very dear in the end."

"On the contrary sir," replied Sean, smiling. "They were the best investment I ever made. I believe they cost you dearer."

"Perhaps you are right at that," said Father, looking at me thoughtfully, then handing me the child, whom I put back in her crib. He went over to Sean, though with great reserve, and shook his hand. "I am very glad to make your acquaintance," he said to him, and Sean replied in kind, as I knew he would.

"I am glad you are here," I told Father, feeling sympathy for the enormous effort he had made, "because you will be able to teach the child my side of her heritage." He looked somewhat relieved after hearing these words, more certain of his reception, and took off his coat, as if he meant to stay.

"Is there any hot water, Rebecca?" he enquired, and I went to place the kettle on the fire.

"I have my own cup outside," said he, as for dietary reasons he couldn't use ours, "and tea leaves. I shall not be gone a minute." But he took even less time than he had promised, returning within ten seconds and almost exploding with anxiety: "In the blessed name of God, what has become of Sarah? She has left the privy, that is certain, for the door hangs open, and as to where she has got to now, Heaven only knows." Running out again to look for her, he almost fell over his trunk and bags in his haste.

"Do not worry, we shall find her by her footprints," I said, going out after him and rushing towards the backhouse, as the snow fell in heavy lumps from the sky. "They will not be hidden yet." In the summer there would be potatoes and squash, cabbage and onions growing in this yard, and Sean and I would almost break our backs digging them up. Now there were only drifts and more drifts, and the intricate pattern of footsteps in the snow.

"I do not doubt it for a second. She is never lost for long," said Father, and I thought I detected a rueful quality to his voice. After all, he had been obliged to keep up with Sarah's variability without help for a year and a half. I counted my blessings that there were now four of us to assist him, rather than my poor sad self as before. "But do you know what, Rebecca?" He stopped for a moment and gazed through the heavy flakes at the vast emptiness outside our cabin, the tiny farms beyond. "Do you know what? I think I shall set up an enterprise here, for I truly do believe I shall have no competition."

"You are entirely right, Father," I replied, smiling at his totally impractical notion and realizing we would have him with us always as part of our family. If a little richer, our lives would definitely be less peaceful. "Nobody has yet considered running a jewellery shop in our community."

Sean, ever thoughtful, brought out Father's coat and my cloak, whilst we stood shivering in the snowy wilderness. I could sense the brooding mountains in the distance, the frozen river nearby. Peggy and Mary joined us and we ran about almost joyfully in the darkness, discovering more footprints and conducting a search for Sarah that would almost certainly prove fruitful. Inside, so loudly that we could hear her above the wind, our baby was chuckling.

About the Author

Lynne Kositsky was born in Montreal and grew up in England. She returned to Canada in 1969 to marry, has three grown children, and lives with her husband in Toronto. Lynne has published a chapbook of poetry, *pcb jam*, and many poems. She has won several awards for her writing, including the E.J. Pratt Award. After many years as a teacher, she decided to start writing for children. *Candles,* her first novel, has been nominated for the Geoffrey Bilson Award for Historical Fiction for Young People, and is on the Canadian Children's Book Centre's *Our Choice* list.

ON TIME'S WING
CANADIAN HISTORICAL FICTION
FROM ROUSSAN

Run for Your Life, Wilma E. Alexander
Living Freight, Barbara Haworth-Attard
Dark of the Moon, Barbara Haworth-Attard
Home Child, Barbara Haworth-Attard
Love-Lies-Bleeding, Barbara Haworth-Attard
Rebecca's Flame, Lynne Kositsky